THE GUEST LECTURE

Also by Martin Riker
Samuel Johnson's Eternal Return

THE GUEST LECTURE

A NOVEL

MARTIN RIKER

Black Cat
New York

FIRST EDITION

Published simultaneously in Canada
Printed in Canada

First Grove Atlantic paperback edition: January 2023

Library of Congress Cataloging-in-Publication data is available for this title.

ISBN 978-0-8021-6041-6
eISBN 978-0-8021-6042-3

Black Cat
an imprint of Grove Atlantic
154 West 14th Street
New York, NY 10011

Distributed by Publishers Group West

groveatlantic.com

23 24 25 26   10 9 8 7 6 5 4 3 2 1

There is no reason why we should not feel ourselves free to be bold, to be open, to experiment, to take action, to try the possibilities of things. And over against us, standing in the path, there is nothing but a few old gentlemen tightly buttoned-up in their frock coats, who only need to be treated with a little friendly disrespect and bowled over like ninepins.

John Maynard Keynes, 1929

THE GUEST LECTURE

A dark hotel room somewhere in middle America. The furniture, which it's too dark to see, includes chairs and small tables, a TV, probably a desk, and a single king-sized bed that currently holds three breathing bodies. On the left lies a man, in the middle a girl, both on their sides and sleeping. On the right: a woman on her back, awake. Her eyes are either open and staring at the ceiling, or else closed; at any given moment, it's one or the other. She lies perfectly still, not making a sound, but inside her head, things are busy. A lecture is about to begin.

1

W alk up to the house, which is my house, and therefore familiar and safe. A place to feel at ease, to the extent that I am ever at ease, to put my cares behind me as I face the front steps of my own house, mine and Ed's and Ali's, though they aren't with me now, or waiting inside either—where should I put them? Someplace nice. Not here in the hotel. Out for ice cream? Why not. And I am alone feeling suddenly overwhelmed and underprepared as I climb the porch steps— one, two, three—having imagined all along I'd be swimming in confidence, but now full up with worry and nerves. Worried that worrying about nervousness will cause nervousness, all that stupid self-conscious stuff you let into your brain that takes over your mindspace and mucks up your mnemonic, derailing your already precariously teetering train of thought.

But no, you will focus.

Picture the porch.

I'm up on it now and in fact I'm not alone because here waiting for me is a familiar face, the kind eyes, horsey features, white push-broom mustache: *it's Keynes*. We haven't officially met, but we've known each other all along, and he's smiling, he's happy to see me. "Abigail," he says, "welcome home. I am Maynard. I was born in Cambridge in 1883 and died in Tilton in 1946. Between those dates I lived an extremely busy life filled with lots of interesting facts and anecdotes which you should feel free, my dear, to sprinkle around like pixie dust as we proceed through the rooms of your very nice house, assigning to each a portion of your speech, or talk, or whatever you're calling it. But dust is a little dry"—he coughs—"even pixie dust is a little dry, and right off you won't want to fill up the air with it. You need a simple introduction, I think." He gives a worried grandpa look. "Have you considered where you might start?"

I take his arm and together we push open the front door.

"Why, of course!" he smiles. "We shall start *in the living room.*"

Picture the living room.

Big, airy, soft gray. Rectangular blue coffee table with the glossy finish that always reminds me of pudding, like its surface is coated with smooth blue pudding. Green couch, a little ratty with wear. Big plants on the floor, smaller plants on the bookshelves. Disheveled shelves, poorly organized, under the stained-glass windows. One of each—a window, a bookshelf—on either side of the fireplace. Utterly derelict fireplace, cobwebs in the wire netting, why have we never cleaned the fireplace? Impressive mantel, though. Broad and white and shelfy, like a glacier. Like the edge of an ancient glacier inching its way into the living room. The mantel clutter-free except for that urn Robert gave us as a wedding gift, tucked back there on the right-hand side. Brown speckled urn, little Grecian handles, *to someday store our ashes*, joked Ed when we opened the box. Which was kind of a sweet thing to say, if you think about it.

"We're in the living room?" asks Keynes.

We're in the living room.

"So start your speech!"

Thanks for inviting me, it's a pleasure to be here, and:

In 1930, with the whole world on the verge of the economic disaster that here in the U.S. we called the Great Depression but which in England they called the Great Slump, a name I've always thought had a playful ring to it—*slump*—though obviously nothing about that situation was playful and my god I am rambling already.

In 1930, with the whole world on the verge of the Great Depression, which in England they called the Great Slump, the British economist John Maynard Keynes, by that time already well known, though not as spectacularly famous as he would eventually become, penned a short article titled "Economic Possibilities for Our Grandchildren," in which he made certain specific predictions about future economic growth. He predicted there would be a lot of it. Keynes had no children of his own, let alone any grandchildren, but his message was really to all the fear-stricken people of England on the cusp of their Great Slump, and his message was: *You don't need to worry so much.*

Of course, when an economist tells you not to worry, you might worry all the more. An economist's "don't worry" usually means something bloodlessly calculated, like "worrying will increase the inclination to hoard currency and decrease spending on consumer goods." Keynes worried about those things, too. But he was before all else a humanist, an old-school liberal pragmatist, who believed in the importance of a stable monetary policy for improving the standard of living, but who condemned the love of money for its own sake as *a somewhat disgusting morbidity*. When he proposed that people not worry, it wasn't to paper over the inequities of a system by which the rich come to control an ever-increasing percentage of the aggregate wealth while the poor are systematically disenfranchised. He was saying that he really didn't think worrying was the right thing to do.

And people were very worried, then. In that sense, it was not so different from today. The *reasons* for worry may have been a little different: there was vast economic inequality and rampant nationalism, but no global environmental crisis, at least not that anyone was paying attention to. But the *amount* of worry was about the same, and the various types of worry as well. There was the *pessimism of the revolutionaries*, as Keynes called it, the worry of those who thought the world so doomed that the only hope was to turn everything upside down. Then there was the *pessimism of the reactionaries*, those who thought the world so doomed that any sort of change at all would send civilization reeling into the abyss. Keynes's reply to both was that actually, in the larger scheme of things, if you stepped back a little and looked at history, at where we've come from and how greatly things have changed, not just in the previous couple of years but over the previous centuries, at the incredible things humans are capable of and the incredible things we have actually *done*, then you would see a world on track to great prosperity. Think how exponentially the standard of living had improved for the average person over just a few hundred years. And weren't the next hundred years likely to see even greater improvements?

And so in this article, "Economic Possibilities for Our Grandchildren," written on the cusp of the worst economic slump of modern times, Keynes predicts that over the following century, owing to advances in technology and accumulated capital, the problems of poverty and hunger, which he calls *the economic problem*, by which he means the struggle of humans to survive, to feed ourselves and clothe ourselves—all these sorts of problems, he says, will be permanently *solved*. Everyone will have more than they need, and will no longer have to work so much, at which point we will all come to realize that *the economic problem*, which humans have always assumed was our number one problem—the reason we spend large chunks of our lives at jobs we often dislike or even despise—we'll see that *this* problem is not our ultimate problem at all. No longer struggling merely to get by, finding ourselves instead with time on our hands, we will at long last recognize humanity's true dilemma, its *permanent problem*, which is—

Ali turns—wakes? No, snugs into the covers. Was I mumbling? I often do and don't realize, catch myself while walking down the street. But I think I'd notice my mumbling in a room as quiet as this. In the dark stillness of a room I can't see but know is still out there, all around me, the carpeting I don't want to set anything down on and the shellacked furniture much uglier than ours. If I can hear Ed breathing, certainly I would hear my own mumbling. And Ali's breathing, little soft puffs.

What time is it, anyway? Don't check, you'll wake her. Light sleeper like her mom. Late. Early. The least you can give her is sleep. The very least a mother can do. Someday, daughter, all this insomnia will be yours (imaginary wide-sweeping arm gesture). Until then, I will do everything in my power to guard your quiet. I will lie still as a mummy. A mommy mummy. British people call their mothers *mummy*. Keynes. Ali. Ed. I will keep my busy thoughts trapped in the dungeon wheel. When we domesticated animals, invented religion, figured out math. Then history kicked in, the dubiously glorious progress of Western recorded history, and innovation slowed way down. After that initial burst of invention, we lived with pretty much the same technologies for thousands of years.

Starting in the sixteenth and seventeenth centuries, though, two things happened: England got rich on gold that Sir Francis Drake stole for Queen Elizabeth, who proceeded to invest it in trade, yielding an income of six and a half percent annually, while scientific breakthroughs led to advances in technology on a scale not seen since those early days of wheels, fire, language, math, religion, and domesticated animals. This technological burst brought a revolution in industrial efficiency, but it also spread—or Keynes predicts it would soon spread— to fields like mining and agriculture. Everywhere production would go up, with far less human effort. This would lead, or was leading, or actually it had already led to a phenomenon Keynes calls *technological unemployment*, a term you and I hear all the time but which Keynes apparently thought would be new enough to his readers that he had to explain it. He admits it's a problem, this 1930s version of the robot-future we're all still freaking out about. He admits there will be "a temporary phase of maladjustment," but it isn't an important part of his argument, because his point is that the moment we're living in, or the moment Keynes was writing in, which from the perspective of *all of human history* is basically the same moment—that this moment is volatile and exciting, a period of uncertainty that will involve growing pains but that will ultimately find us in a more mature stage of human existence. The financial catastrophe of 1930 would be a bother, a bad day in a long week, but at its far end lay tremendous widespread prosperity, and in a hundred years, your real problem will be that you're bored. The *permanent problem* is not poverty or scarcity or robots. The permanent problem is life.

He talks about how hard it will be, in a work-free world, for ordinary people to adjust. How both nature and culture have taught us to derive our sense of purpose through *work*, and how for most people, leisure, too, will have to be learned, slowly and over time. "How to occupy the leisure." Leisure as occupation. Finding meaning in a jobless life.

He says it's not just an adjustment to a new way of life but a realignment of values bred into us over countless generations. Money, in particular, will become less important to us. We'll understand that money was never important in itself, that it was only ever important in relation to our needs.

He delineates two *kinds* of needs. Absolute needs are the ones that can be adequately filled: food, shelter. Relative needs are the things you think you need in order to make yourself feel superior to other people: giant cars, designer clothes, the greener grass over the proverbial fence, or whatever the proverbial Joneses have gotten up to. Those wants *masquerading* as needs, he admits, will never go away. It's only real needs we won't have to worry about.

He anticipates the craft craze of the 1950s and the "slow" movements of today. Home-brewed beer. Farm-to-table. The arts of living. An existential turn toward culture. A radical undoing of the division of labor, which since the days of Adam Smith has made our society so efficient but our occupations so drab.

"We shall do more things for ourselves than is usual with the rich today."

In fact, the rich man of his day, the sort of person who already enjoyed the economic freedom Keynes's essay was describing, seemed to Keynes a bad example of the people we would become. The rich man of his day still saw money as an end, not a means, and found meaning in a constantly deferred future rather than the here and now. "For him jam is not jam unless it is a case of jam to-morrow and never jam to-day," Keynes says, paraphrasing one of the queens in one of the Lewis Carroll books. Whereas we, his presumptive grandchildren, will find meaning in life itself. We will become better people and learn to help each other more.

Of course, it seems more than a little idealistic from where you and I are sitting. The obvious rejoinder is that today we are close to *reaching* the one-hundred-year deadline for the utopian predictions John Maynard Keynes made in 1930, and looking around I don't think many of us would claim that *what to do with our free time* is the greatest crisis human beings currently—what? Too long?

Keynes, seated on my living room sofa, has made a face.

"You need to stick to only the most relevant points or this talk will go on forever. On the one hand, you're jumping around too much for a listener to fully appreciate my essay or its various points. On the other, there is much more detail already than you need for your own argument, given that this is only the living room and we have, what, five, six more rooms to go? Plus time for a Q&A. Largely, the problem is that you held off preparing until the very last minute, your infamous procrastination, so instead of a carefully plotted progression, you are following only a hazy outline, stringing together bits and bobs of passages remembered from your book. Quoting yourself and others. Now, Abigail, don't get worked up. I'm not telling you anything you don't know. You've always been overly reactive, and always wished you were less so, but none of that wishing has made the slightest bit of difference, when push comes to shove. Tomorrow, let's face it, won't go very well. It won't go *badly*, but in case it does: Who cares? What does it matter? Well, it matters *to you*. Okay. Better to be a person who cares about things than a person who doesn't. Better still to care but not lose sleep over it. The lengthy history lesson, at least, needs to go. Personally, I would keep the line about me sounding like a prophet rather than an economist, then cut to those hundred years being now nearly past, then say something simple like: 'To put it in Keynesian terms, *the economic problem* has not been solved.'"

Understatement it is, then.

In fact, *the economic problem* is so far from being solved that most of Keynes's predictions seem, from the perspective of today—ridiculous? Naïve? Or, *or*, we might be misunderstanding the lesson of "Economic Possibilities for Our Grandchildren"—and this is what I wish to speak about today. About optimism and pragmatism, about reality and storytelling, about being "right" versus being "useful," and what all these things have to do with how we think and talk in our own day and age. Keynes himself, when he made his predictions, said his forecast for humanity depended upon some important practical caveats, such as there not being any more major wars or much growth in population. I think we can all agree this describes very poorly the situation we've experienced since 1930, which of course Keynes had no way of foreseeing.

"Except that I predicted World War II."

Except that he warned, in the wake of World War I, that harsh reparations against the Germans would end badly, would crush the German economy and cripple their ability to pay, and would therefore be both impractical and dangerous, leading to deepening resentment and a reescalation of tensions. In other words, yes, he predicted World War II.

"That was in 1919," adds Keynes, who's looking very comfortable on my slightly ratty green sofa. He is too much the gentleman to rest his feet on the coffee table, but he leans back with his long thin legs crossed, not the intense posture and expression I imagine he perpetually struck in real life but rather a picture of ease, a pastoral Keynes, like a character out of *The Wind in the Willows*. Would Keynes have read *The Wind in the Willows*? He liked Lewis Carroll, but Carroll is a different sort of English sensibility. Math and light melancholy, playfulness and possibility. Wry wit. Grahame is weightier, more sentiment-heavy, though line for line the better writer, I think. Less clever but more convincing. Ali prefers him. She likes Mr. Toad. What do I mean by "convincing"?

Anyway, Keynes, I'm glad to see you making yourself at home. I was starting to wish I'd never agreed to this whole "loci" method—which was Ed's idea, by the way, back when the invitation for this talk came in. He was rereading Cicero, working on I-don't-know-what, he doesn't always tell me what he's working on. But the invitation asked for a talk, not a paper, they seemed very concerned that I would put them through a PowerPoint presentation—well, I probably would have—and Ed said, You know, it always impresses people when you wing it. Wing it? When you know your stuff so entirely you can just talk. The logical fallacy *there* being, I replied, that just because a person "knows her stuff," therefore she will be able to "wing it," as if everybody who knows their stuff also has the gift of effortless gab, as if the source of all oratorical effortlessness is simply the knowing of one's stuff and has nothing to do with actual skill in public speaking. At which point Ed, lacking a compelling counterargument, but fascinated as usual with his own pet interests, said, You know what? You should use the *loci method*. Then he hauled out again that story about the ancient Greek banquet and the poet whose name I can never remember. Simon something.

Simonides.

Simonides of Ceos.

Once upon a time, Simonides of Ceos, a poet who lived so long ago that he actually invented several letters of the Greek alphabet, was at a banquet, a swanky affair. At some point in the evening he was called outside, maybe he needed to pee, I don't remember, but while he was gone the roof collapsed and killed everyone. The bodies were too mangled to identify—*lovely story, Ed*—but Simonides of Ceos pulled an interesting trick: by mentally imagining himself moving around the room, he was able to recall all of the people in the order in which they'd been seated. And a colleague of his, or just someone who was listening, and who was apparently unfazed by the gruesome backstory, realized this would be a great way to remember a speech. You assign a different portion of the speech to each room of a building you know well, then you mentally move through this building as you go, remembering each speech portion by picturing yourself in the room you put it in. Thus out of the ruins of the worst party ever—says Ed—came a method of memorization taught by Cicero and Quintilian and practiced by lawyers and politicians for hundreds of years.

We were in this very living room when he said that, Keynes. The actual room in my house, I mean. I was pacing and Ed was sitting right where you're sitting now, and I said, *Okay*. I said, Sure, let's try it. Why? Because back then tomorrow's talk was still far off in the distance. *Back then* my life and career prospects were all sunshine and promises, not the devastated wasteland that stretches before me tonight. Back then my party was hopping, the roof seemed imperviously sturdy—Abigail was on the rise! A force to be reckoned with, full of confidence or hubris or at the very least indifference to a far-off lecture for a bunch of people I didn't know, who I didn't even have a particularly good sense of, in terms of their interests in general or in me in particular, just that they liked "talks," but nothing too technical, not a paper I would give to colleagues, and who also—these mysterious people—differed from my colleagues in that once my talk was over, I would never see them again. The future seemed chock-full of such speaking engagements *back then*, Keynes, speaking engagements as far as the eye could see. And there was Ed saying, *It always impresses people when you wing it.* There was me thinking, *How bad could it be?*

But it's lonely, is what I didn't expect. Even with Ali and Ed right here. Lying in the dark in this shitty hotel, proceeding in my mind through my imaginary house, imagining myself talking to empty rooms, to no one. Did Cicero never consider how lonely that is? Weren't any of those hundreds of years' worth of lawyers and politicians ever bothered by this? But with you along, Keynes—this was what I started off to say— with you along, I have to admit, I feel much better about it.

"You get to show me around."

I do.

"You've always felt a special affection for me."

2

A tall room with good windows. The only piece of art is Ed's forest landscape painting, which he brought into our marriage from some unascertainable previous moment in his life, and which he does not claim is great *art*, he just *likes* it. Giant funereal sideboard inherited from Ed's family—not a treasured heirloom, his mom bought it at a flea market—that in any other room would look like a set prop for *The Addams Family* but in this room really works, somehow. Next, the table with its diagonal legs. I suppose they look stylish, but they make it very awkward to seat more than four people. A Persian rug. When did we get that? Threadbare, needs replacing, but I like it anyway. I like the rocks and the trinkets arranged on the windowsill. I like the hardwood floor. I like the stained-glass window identical to the two in the living room. The fake-wood ceiling fan left over from the previous homeowner I do *not* particularly like, but then, how often do I look up? This whole room, I like. The living room, too, back when we were standing over there. My house.

I wish I were really in those rooms right now, one of those rooms instead of this one. This whole hotel smells like laundry. No, like a smell sprayed from a can. That time Ali and I were in line at the pharmacy and saw, on a storage shelf over the cashier's shoulder, a cardboard box labeled "Farts in a Can" and "Made in China"—because they sell a lot of gag gifts in that place. Me of course thinking instantly about all the waste, the environmental cost of shipping consumerist crap from China, the Texas-sized trash heap in the middle of the Pacific, and how my daughter's generation will never know the sense of well-being my own took for granted, the limitless security we felt but never realized we were feeling. Silently thinking all that but actually *saying* to her, to be funny, to keep it upbeat: *Those farts came all the way from China.*

But Ali, serious-faced: Who made them?

Some factory.

No, who *made* them?

Oh, who *made* them. Beats me!

Then a fidgety sort of silence, until out in the car she started rattling them off, old people and young, rich and poor, tall and short, one by one, all the different people she'd imagined in China who had taken time out of their busy days to fart into those cans in our pharmacy. That was only a couple of years ago. She's still little. Still mine. Actually, this room doesn't smell so bad. It doesn't smell like much of anything.

Nor is it noisy, exactly—you are a blessing, my quiet sleepers—but nois*es*, yes. There's no such thing as true silence. John Cage once climbed into a sensory deprivation tank and came out later announcing that there's no such thing as true silence as long as you're alive, because you can always hear your own heartbeat. To experience absolute silence, you'd need to be dead. Tonight, I appear to be more alive than is strictly necessary, my heartbeat is *very* loud, not just in my chest but in my head, my ears. I can *feel* it beating. But I am also calm. I feel wired and calm at the same time, the mind busy but the body stuck. Is it nerves or anxiety? Nerves would just be about the talk tomorrow. Anxiety would be about everything else. Maybe it's different feelings causing separate effects, like getting poison ivy on top of chicken pox. My heartbeat is the loudest sound in my head, when I stop talking to myself. It isn't the loudest sound in the room, though. Outside my head, you can't hear it.

In the room, three distinct sounds are layered one atop the other, occurring simultaneously but with no real connection. The high one is electronic. It's coming from the television or the phone. The middle one, the loudest and most complicated, is the air-conditioning. It's more of a tinny rattle. The low one is unplaceable, a sort of ubiquitous whimper that is not even inside this room but more like a sound the building makes, as if the building itself is moaning. Or maybe it's the sound of all the other rooms, the accumulated white noise of all those sleeping strangers, their specific snores and grunts and coughs and rolling-overs and pillow-flips and blanket-yanking not *singularly* audible in here, thank goodness, but taken together forming a pervasive human rumble, a collective ambient grumble, the nocturnal soundtrack of this cheapish hotel.

It's a little surprising, frankly. The honorarium's not bad, which means they have money to spend, and also suggests they want to make their speakers happy, because who knows, they might want to invite us back, or else one speaker might talk to another—surely there's some sort of speaker circuit and they all talk to one another—and they wouldn't want one saying, *The fee's good but they're surprisingly stingy with the accommodations*. Not that I'm some kind of superstar, probably to them I'm a B-lister, a brown dwarf, but still, it makes a difference, the sort of room you're in. It shapes your whole mood.

Like that Christmas when the basement flooded. Not a flake of snow, but rain for *days and days*, and Ali and I were playing Connect Four at the dining room table when we heard a giant crash, then an enormous rushing *gush*, like the whole house had just gone over the edge of Niagara Falls. Ali jumped, I shouted, and Ed came bounding down from upstairs straight to the basement. The storm drain in the alley had gotten clogged with leaves, which caused water from all the way up the block to pour into our backyard and blow the basement door right off its hinges. You could hear it rushing in. Ed was shouting that he couldn't stop it, Ali was freaking out, so after calling 911 I ran her over to the neighbors, then went back to find Ed in the backyard, in freezing water a foot deep, using a rake and a broom to prop the patio table sideways at the top of the outside stairwell, to divert the incoming water around the side of the house. Then the firemen showed up. They stood out there in the rain, five or six big men in their rubber uniforms, staring at Ed's patio-table contraption, until one of them shrugs and says, *That's about as good as anything we could do.* I was flabbergasted. Ed was clearly proud of himself. Finally, the friendly house inspector arrived and very apologetically *condemned our house,* because the firemen had turned off the gas and apparently there's an ordinance. *Just a temporary condemning* but he had to put that bright orange shaming sticker on a street-facing window, he tried to pick a spot that was hidden by a bush, but still, how humiliating. Plus then you have to vacate until all the water's out.

So we booked a room at the nice hotel down the street, the one that always looked so charming: not overly fancy, but cozy and clean. Ed took Ali swimming in the indoor pool. I treadmilled in the little gym. I was sweating out my frustration, starting to feel better, when that horrible face came on the giant TV screen, and the *voice*. It was just after the election, he wasn't even in office yet, but already his voice was all over the place, it was everywhere. I'd been staying away from TVs all month trying to hide from it. Just the *thought* that I'd have to hear it now, over and over, that we'd all be forced to listen to it, what an awful thought, don't think about this, why did I want to think about *this*? Oh, because later, after we'd showered and put on pj's, and crawled into bed and talked about our crazy day, and ordered room service that came on a cart, on plates with plastic covers, and Ali got to choose which one of us to sleep with and she chose me, at that point I *did* feel better. A lot better. That night in that nice hotel room, in the midst of that terrible day when all those awful things had happened, I felt better than I'd felt in a very long time.

"With all due respect," says Keynes, who's been standing all this while in the space between the window and Ed's landscape painting, a spot that in real life is home to a leafy tall floor plant that I for some reason forgot to picture a moment ago when I was taking myself around the dining room—well, I guess Keynes is there now—"With all due respect," he says, "the point of Cicero's loci method seems a little lost on you."

I *am* wandering. At least I'm calm. I'm frankly impressed by how calm I'm keeping. I don't always, Keynes. It must be your influence. Anyway, what's the hurry? I think we'll be awake for a while.

"But if your intention is to mentally rehearse tomorrow's talk, which does seem like a very good use of your insomnia, then shouldn't you proceed as closely as possible to how you'd like this talk to actually go?"

Where was I.

"You've looked all around the dining room. You've set me down in a spot usually reserved for a houseplant, but everything else is per usual. You are feeling very happy to be here, content, as the next portion of your speech—in which you discuss the ways my essay was wrong, and why it was wrong, and why it was perhaps never intended to be right—as all of that comes flowing back to you . . ."

But before we start talking about what "Economic Possibilities for Our Grandchildren" might teach us about living in this current day and age—not about whether Keynes was right but whether he's useful, and how being useful might be a way of being right—before we head in that direction, we should first take a closer look at the various ways he was certainly wrong. These we can divide, to make them easier for me to remember and to create the illusion that this talk has been carefully organized, into two types. Two categories of wrongness. He was wrong because of his own shortcomings, and he was wrong because of ours.

To understand *his* shortcomings, you need to know something about his life, the Victorian and Edwardian worlds in which he lived, in which his morals and his desires and his cares and beliefs were formed, though that could easily be a lecture all its own, or series of lectures, none of which would be the pithy upbeat presentation I am supposed to be giving you people, a talk about optimism at a time when I am personally feeling anything but. When I have been stripped of my own optimism by recent life events that I am *not* going to think about now. No, I am not. No, I am *not*. Except perhaps just to acknowledge the irony, that here I am serving myself up as some sort of expert on how to proceed through the world with intention and purpose when in fact I am utterly lost. When everything I have ever worked for is STOP. Just stop.

"Tell me, again," Keynes—my conscience, maybe—changes the subject, "why they need to know my shortcomings?"

Because I don't want to pretend you were some kind of saint.

"Yes, but why bother saying much about *me* at all?"

Why? Why.

Because my whole talk hangs on the idea that your essay was fundamentally a rhetorical and imaginative gesture. Because the point I'll be coming to is that you were more interested in proposing a utopian space for thinking through how the world *could be different* than in fastidiously predicting what would actually come to pass. And if that's my point, if what I'm arguing is your *intent*, then it would help if my audience had a sense of who you were. Because the *person you were* says a lot about how you saw the world, the ethics behind your economics, the importance you placed on public discourse, the importance you placed on all kinds of things. But if I just list off your accomplishments, I risk making you out to be some sort of romanticized unproblematic magical guru-person, effectively undermining the very pragmatism, the pragmatic optimism, that by the end I'll be arguing is the true lesson of your essay, if not your life. Because it's not really about you, Keynes. It's about the ways you managed to be better than yourself. They need to know your shortcomings because that's what makes you human, and your humanity is a large part of why you're worth talking about at all. Okay?

"It's off subject," says Keynes plainly. "You'll run out of time."

Well, let's see how much I can even remember.

He was in some ways the very model of the liberal English gentleman, raised in the Victorian era, not from a wealthy family but certainly not from a poor one. Hardworking. Self-driven. Tall, gawky. Sickly? It seems like every famous intellectual in history spent their childhood sickly. But Keynes eventually died of being sickly. Died younger than usual, I mean. Obviously, lots of people die of being sickly.

A healthy ego, anyway, alpha child, best boy, a winner in all the ways that might make a parent proud. He was the sort of young man who cares about pleasing his parents. This brisk "winning" youth blossoming, then, into an intellectual and artistic young adulthood: model student, debate club, a predilection for theater, performed on stage at Eton, bit of a ham. Perhaps most importantly for our purposes today, this tall gawky young man, who would someday invent macro-economics, adamantly refused to specialize in *math*, despite the considerable pressure, from various directions, that came with being incredibly good at it. Because he was also good at, and interested in, so many other things.

Bearing in mind that economics, back then, was not as math-frenzied as it is today. When Keynes came to it, economics was still a branch of moral philosophy. The author of *The Wealth of Nations* had also written *The Theory of Moral Sentiments*. Moral sentiments! Would that more of my own colleagues took up the study of *those*. Keynes did *study* math, of course. He liked math. But he also liked medieval poetry. And classical opera. And contemporary art. All of which seems relevant to the person he was, and why he thought in the ways he thought, but you're right this is probably already too much detail for tomorrow.

"Very probably," says imaginary Keynes, now seated at my dining room table, having grabbed a deck of cards from the sideboard drawer, and shuffling. "I think, Abigail, as a general rule, in every instance and in all places, you should talk only an eighth as long as you feel like you want to. An eighth at the very most. No one will notice what you've left out, because it will never have been there in the first place, and your listeners will attend to your words better if the words themselves are fewer. You were born into an era of overload. Leaving things out is the great unmastered art form of your age."

His bohemian arty side, on the other hand, is extremely relevant and just too interesting to bypass entirely, and if nothing else tomorrow's audience of—retirees? homemakers?—will depart having learned something about the Bloomsbury group, some bits and bobs of history, something tangible, take-away-able, the satisfaction of a knowable thing. For example, the bizarre and wonderful factoid that Keynes was housemates with Virginia Woolf. They were friends and she at some point claimed to be jealous that he could do what she did—write beautifully—but she couldn't do what he did—economics, politics. His influential position at the center of both intellectual and artistic culture in early twentieth-century England. The story of how he bought a newspaper, *The Nation and Athenaeum*, that became a megaphone for Liberal politics and economics but also a platform for Modernist artists and writers. He even tried to hire T. S. Eliot—whose famous poem *The Waste Land* was inspired by one of Keynes's economics tracts, no I am not kidding—as *The Nation*'s literary editor, but Eliot turned out to be a real handful, so Keynes offered the job instead to Virginia's husband, Leonard.

And philosophers! He was friends with Bertrand Russell and Ludwig Wittgenstein, and was instrumental in getting the *Tractatus Logico-Philosophicus* published while Wittgenstein was in a POW camp in Italy. The *Tractatus* being the book that effectively founded analytic philosophy, and in doing so put Keynes's own budding philosophy career out of business. His close but complicated relationship with Lytton Strachey. His long romantic relationship with the painter Duncan Grant, left out of the pages of Keynes's first biography for presumably political reasons, probably also left out of my talk tomorrow, because I'd have no idea how to bring it up without sounding like I'm making some big deal of it. Eventually he surprised his friends by marrying Lydia Lopokova, a Russian superstar ballerina he fell in love with while she was performing in Diaghilev's *Sleeping Beauty*. She traveled with him to international economics conferences and met all the leading math nerds of their age. They were devoted to each other. In their later years, they lived in the country with dogs and housekeepers and kept mostly to themselves.

And after he got rich, which he did by writing internationally bestselling books but also through successful market speculation, he became a great art collector and patron, particularly of his Bloomsbury friends. He founded the Cambridge Arts Theatre, and was instrumental in establishing government arts funding in England. He did more for the arts on a volunteer basis than most artists manage in their lifetimes, all while working in government, and shaping British economic policy, and meeting with world leaders to plan the economic resolutions of World Wars I and II, and founding both the International Monetary Fund and the World Bank, and holding various academic positions, and reconfiguring the theory and practice of economics in the twentieth century, and walking his dogs, and—how am I doing?

"Other than it being twenty times too long?"

Other than that.

"Fine. Though I can't say I've noticed anything yet that would obviously qualify as a 'shortcoming.'"

Getting there!

Now, I have no idea if any of those names will mean anything to you, ladies and gentlemen. The larger point I'm making is simply that Keynes was both an intellectual and artistic soul, and his idea of the "good life," the one he imagined us all happily attaining, was based on the life he personally knew. A champion of the economic underdog, of prosperity for everyone, he was, like the rest of Bloomsbury, culturally a bit of a snob. More Liberal than Labour, where culture was concerned. Which becomes a shortcoming when it leads him to presume, in "Economic Possibilities for Our Grandchildren"— you see? back to the subject—that we all desire the lifestyles of cultured British white people; that the whole world aspires to the same sort of society and economy and holds similar values and beliefs. For example, the belief that *not working* is something everyone should want. Not all of us share that particular view. *Some* of us can imagine nothing better than keeping our jobs—in fact at the moment, "leisure" sounds to me rather like another word for *doom*, for *failure*, though obviously I will not get into any of that tomorrow, nothing about myself or my problems. None of you know me, and even if you did, you couldn't possibly understand. I would sound like a crazy person!

I am not a crazy person, ladies and gentlemen, at least I don't think of myself as a crazy person, but I am also not sure that I am any *better* of a person, any taller in my shortcomings, than the dead British man I've chosen to keep me company, not just tonight but over the course of my—I almost said "my career." Keynes was a privileged member of a colonizing capitalist nation who loved his way of life, was generally proud of his country's place in history, and presumed to impose his own ideas of happiness on others, but is Abigail any better? I've struggled with the same questions—how the world should change, how changes should be made, what a better world would look like—and I suspect my answers are just as limited by my own values, my assumptions, the biases I don't even see, the personal deficiencies I try not to think about.

The other day in the kitchen, for example, I was listening to the radio, a conversation about race and whiteness, and whoever was speaking suddenly asked the audience to ask themselves, "How many Black friends do you have?" At first the question bugged me, a knee-jerk irritation, not because I don't have African American friends, I thought—it's just condescending to tally it up like that. But then I thought, *There's a point being made, an important point, okay.* A few colleagues from other departments; four or five parents from Ali's school; friends in college, summer jobs; and plenty of students, if students can count as friends. That was the question, really: what counts as a "friend"? At which point the radio guest added, as if they'd heard my question, or maybe the interviewer had actually asked it, "I mean someone you've eaten at least two meals with." I tried to remember the last time I'd gone out with anyone other than Ed, then made two terrible realizations: that I have no Black friends, and that I don't seem to have any friends at all.

The big difference, then, the saving difference, though it is not a very saving difference, it is more like a sad pathetic difference, but the *defining* difference between my shortcomings and Keynes's is that mine have hardly ever imposed themselves on anyone. My ideas have not remade economic theory, or settled geopolitical disputes, or helped establish international cooperative monetary oversight institutions. My prejudices and presumptions have had pitifully little effect on anything at all. So I guess there's that to feel good about.

Another fun fact that is not actually fun: he was anti-Semitic, in the insidiously casual way that "everyone was back then." Leonard Woolf must have put up with a lot from his Bloomsbury friends. At least Keynes hated Hitler. Hated fascism.

What was my other category? *Our* shortcomings.

Oh boy.

Freed of the burden of work, we would all learn to love the finer things, the gifts of education and art. Scarcity would be eradicated, rich countries would share with poorer countries, and before you knew it, everyone would be fed, housed, clothed, and off to the English countryside, messing about in boats. For those who like work, well, leisure can be a kind of work. They would pursue the work that brought pleasure, rather than the work that was just a job. The whole world would be finished with "just a job." We could all find our true callings, and would come to judge the quality of our lives, not in dollars and possessions, but in how our time is spent. When you put it that way, it does sound pretty good.

But he failed to foresee our shortcomings. Presumably he did not actually believe the next hundred years would be free of wars and population growth, but he had no way of knowing, for example, that TV would arrive, filling our days with its nonsense. Then the internet. How mass psychological manipulation by the advertising industry would amp up the consumerist side of our natures, causing us to care so much more and so vapidly about what other people have. The rampant increase in per capita consumption. The endless distractions of modern life. The rise of the military-industrial complex and how it would soak up our surpluses in the accumulation of weapons of mass destruction. Of weapons of any size of destruction. He did not foresee the "Great Acceleration," which only really got going after he died. The explosive expansion not just of technology but of all kinds of Earth-altering activities, how capitalism would reshape the planet, the environmental and social and economic costs that climate catastrophe would impose unequally but without exception around the world. The down-the-road consequences of endless growth. How the income inequality caused by globalization would render traditional political structures increasingly susceptible to the very sort of authoritarian takeover bids that keep popping up these days. Attacks on democracy! Two whole years, now, of that hideous man and his ghoulish cronies. Two years of terrifying obviousness, of conspiracy theories and white

Even the kids all seemed to know each other. The hallway so full of people it was hard to move around and I couldn't stand it, I couldn't breathe. I mean, I could *breathe*, but it felt like I was stuffed inside of something. I said to myself, *All your childhood up through high school you're packed in with these people who have nothing to do with you or how you think. Who seem so much surer of themselves and their place in the world than you ever feel . . . At last you go to college and into adulthood and you're free of those people, you find people more like you . . . But then you have a kid and she has to go to school, and suddenly you're surrounded by them again, the high school people, not the same people but close enough, with their own confident kids who your kid is packed in with*—snarky thoughts that were unfair to those people, since how do I know what they're like or what they're thinking? But there was a bigger picture there that no one was acknowledging. That's what was upsetting me. My snarky thoughts were meant to distract me from the bigger picture, because the full picture is always paralyzing. Ed must have noticed since he pulled me aside. What was I going to do, homeschool? I don't know, is that an option? He tried reminding me that we were kids once too, we'd handled that same mess, he and I had both survived kindergarten, and Ali's so much better than us. She might be better, I said, but the world's so much worse! Domestic insecurity, social insecurity, digital insecurity, climate insecurity, or rather *crisis*, climate crisis, racial crisis, moral crisis, midlife crisis—I didn't say these things to Ed but I was thinking them. Financial crisis, energy crisis, housing crisis, healthcare crisis—it was one of my toughest days, having to let her go like that. Arms race, tech race, wage gap, food desert, class action—this was back around the time I stopped driving, back when I wrote the essay, but I remember the scene like it was yesterday: the names were called and the kids lined up, Ali was smiling and everybody was happy and I'm there thinking *factory farming strip mining clear cutting reef bleaching.* Of course I have tough days all the time, and tough nights, I never remember them, I just move on, but you can't move on from everything, sometimes you have to arrive, and that day was different, a memory. One of those moments in life when the consequences of your choices are set out in front of you, and so are everyone else's. Everyone is watching with total attention as the consequences of their choices line up to go inside the classroom and everyone's happy, even I was happy, I was maybe the happiest I have ever been, and proud, *so* proud, but I was also *Armageddon,* I was *overpopulation species-extinction* breathe—

Breathe.

Okay.

Ed had no idea how dark things got that day. He doesn't know what's going on with me half the time. If half the time he knew half the things I was thinking, he'd decide I was crazy or else give me a medal for holding it together at all.

I'm sorry that Ed has to do all the driving now, I do feel bad about that, but guilt aside, thinking only about driving and the fact that I no longer do it, I couldn't be happier. Everybody should stop driving. Everybody should get Ed to drive them wherever they need to go. He's a pretty good driver, though he does lose his temper. He yells at stoplights. It's funny, since he's such a calm person otherwise. Set him at a really long red, though, or in front of anybody riding his tail, or behind anybody driving slower than the speed limit, and suddenly he's throwing up his arms and cursing, his pathetic displays of rage, *damn shit fuck damn*, even with Ali right there in the back seat. On second thought, maybe Ed is not the right person to drive America.

"Probably not."

Keynes! You're supposed to be keeping me on track.

"Yes, well." He's looking at his card game. He picks up a column from the right and places it at the bottom of a column in the middle. "The problem, I think," he says, "is that it is very difficult for you to focus, here in the dining room of your mind. What I mean is, you are having a hard time remaining here, with me and with your speech, when you know very well that you are actually out there, in the world of problems. How to stay on track when the only thing standing between the two of us and that tinny air conditioner are the four walls of your skull and the thin scrim of your imagination."

I actually do need to practice, though. And I do *not* want to think about anything related to politics, or income inequality, climate catastrophe, nothing to do with my house, my family, my utterly devastated career prospects, or anything at all like that. How the future keeps promising horrific possibilities. How the horrors have already started arriving. How the horrors are like a dinner guest who shows up twenty minutes earlier than you were expecting them, when you're not done cooking, so they sit there hovering as you go on trying to pretend it's all normal and fine. Your life. Your failure. Your daughter's future. Those are the *last* thoughts I need right now. But they're so abundant, Keynes! They're everywhere, those thoughts. The very air this brain breathes. I could try all night to avoid them, but they'd still come around knocking like a thousand times.

Knock

knock

knock

knock

knock

knock

3

"**O**rder in the court! Order in the court!"

Stifled hubbub. Papers shuffled. Muffled grousing.

I am in the witness box, seated in a large chair between low walls of ornately carved wood, a spot of grandeur in this mostly austere—but large, packed, a seemingly random assembly of anonymous onlookers—municipal courtroom. Slightly to my right, a line of old men stare at me from the far side of a similarly ornate wooden table. Their expressions are dour, their faces ancient, sunken, like portraits on loan from the attic of Dorian Gray. Now and then, one of them wheezes out some fusty rule or rotten intellection, poisoning the air with the rarified mouth-stench unique to this species, the smugly entrenched academic.

Am I really going to go here? Just because certain personal realities are very powerful and keep resurfacing as you lie motionless in the dark, and take over your imagination and fill it with thoughts you would rather not think, that doesn't mean you *have* to think those thoughts, or are entirely powerless to avoid them.

You are not entirely powerless.

But mostly, yes, you are powerless.

"Am I to understand"—Keynes, now dressed in British tweed, stands casually but with poise in the carpeted space between my box and their table—"that these gentlemen seated before you, whom until recently you counted as *colleagues*, and who in theory, if not in practice, counted you the same, that this grumbling line of bitter visages not only voted against your tenure application at the department level, effectively ensuring your dismissal from the university and instantly transforming you into the academic equivalent of 'damaged goods,' such that finding a position elsewhere will be ten times harder than if you'd never taken that job in the first place, in effect sending you and your family into the proverbial street—not, of course, in the way that people less fortunate than you get sent into the actual street, which is a lot of people, around the world and in your own community, so many people in situations so much worse than yours that anyone with a conscience, finding themselves in your position, would probably feel ashamed for worrying about themselves or ever complaining about anything—except that it's scary, yes. You're allowed to feel scared. All those years of work only to find yourself stranded without career or plans or prospects— Am I to understand," Keynes collects himself, "that these men not only denied you tenure, but that you actually believe they never intended to support you *in the first place?*"

That is correct.

Gasps!

This isn't even what a real courtroom is like.

"And what evidence can you cite to support this claim?"

Well, everything, right? The way they looked down at me, the way they spoke down to me, *when* they spoke to me, their wildly inappropriate comments on my appearance—*What happened to you?* being easily the most memorable, since I didn't even know what that referred to, and spent the rest of the day trying to figure out what was wrong with my hair or outfit. Or the litany of nasty looks the one time I wore gym clothes in the department office. I wasn't even teaching that day, just making copies, if there wasn't always such a line for the copy machine, I wouldn't have had to squeeze it in. Not to mention all the meetings and student gatherings the older faculty skipped. All the grad students I had to advise, which is extra work I was *not* supposed to be given, but the students asked for me, they specifically requested me, not that I blame them, the students like me and I like them, *teaching* I like, working with students, a fact my colleagues were more than happy to exploit, knowing of course that all that extra work would count for nothing, tenure-wise. All the interstitial extras that never counted for anything, tenure-wise. How they turned every day into a test. How any time I would successfully fulfill some expectation, they would add others on top of it, like a boss who can't even keep track of all the meaningless crap he's asked you to do. How they kept upping the expectations and darkening the forecast, so that the more I did, and the further I advanced, the less likely it seemed that I would ever arrive.

"They pushed, pushed, pushed," offers Keynes, "while at the same time they discouraged, they condescended, they picked apart."

Which for the longest time I convinced myself was a sort of tough love, you know? As if secretly they were just trying to make me stronger, my CV more ironclad. For the longest time I held on to this illusion, maybe because Ed kept telling me that *had* to be it, that there was no way they were actually this horrible, because why would they hire me and start me on the tenure track in the first place if they only wanted me to fail? And I said, No, it's only because Maggie was there and she was looking out for me. She was the one who got me the job, but then she left. She pulled me in the door on her way out. But Ed countered that one person alone can't get you a job, not in academia anyway. Academia is all about committees. It's where committees go to die, or where people go to die in committee. And I said, Maybe, okay, but what if Maggie cashed in her chips? Over the course of her career she'd put up with so much from them, the only woman in an all-male department. She'd accumulated so many chips on her shoulder, and they knew it. They knew her shoulder was stacked with chips and they knew what they had done to put them there. Maybe the chips on Maggie's shoulder were stacked in my favor? Even back then I understood this. Even back then I said this to Ed. Her last act as an academic was to muscle me in, then she packed up and moved to New Zealand. Mic drop. I was Maggie's Obamacare. Disgruntled incumbents started dismantling me the minute she was out the door.

But Ed couldn't get his head around that, so I couldn't really get my head around it either. That people could actually be that way, not just in government but in actual life. We couldn't believe anyone would want to devote such purely destructive energy to . . . well, anything. That even with the discourse having shifted and despite whatever progress has been made, in an academic culture of heightened awareness and accountability, of student demonstrations, rescinded invitations, and faculty diversity training, at the end of the day, it's still just angry old men marking their territory. We were sheep, you see, trusting sheep. Is that why Trump became president? Because people like Ed and me were raised to be sheep?

"Or because people like *them* were raised to be wolves," offers Keynes, indicating my ex-colleagues, who make aghast faces but basically just have to sit there and take it, because this is *my* imagination, assholes.

You know what being on the tenure track was like, Keynes? I had this realization the other day. Being on the tenure track was like having Obama for president. There were global terrors and political unrest and social injustice, the world was its usual mess, and worse underneath than anyone realized—but it still felt like we were working *toward* something. Toward safety, and open-mindedness, and security. And that's tenure: the job you love that's yours forever, the stability and freedom from worry that allows you to think creatively, to challenge the status quo, to embrace the utopic potential of the imagination to fundamentally rethink economics, or political science, or the shape of human society, or whatever. And Obama was the promise of that for *everybody*. I mean, he wasn't, of course, not really, but at the time, just having Obama there felt like its own sort of security blanket. Tenure for everybody! A safe and healthy future for everybody! Whereas being denied tenure was Trump. Suddenly we're out on our butts. I'm out on my butt. The world of security and possibility falls away and we're plunged into a new Dark Ages where nothing is stable, nothing is good, where anything good we may have put into the world up to this moment is now meaningless, pointless, *gone*. Where the imagination, wellspring of optimism and possibility, has turned on itself, and now spends all its time obsessing and making everything worse.

"So you jumped all the hurdles," Keynes brings us back. "You sat on all those committees, served as academic advisor to a small army of undergraduates, as faculty advisor for student organizations no one else wanted to advise. You went to lectures your colleagues skipped, attended the poorly attended parties. God help you, you schmoozed. Most importantly of all, the only thing that academia truly seems to care about: you published! For three years you churned out peer-reviewed articles at the expected rate of one per year in Tier 2 journals whose impact factors were within the acceptable range, after which something happened that took your work in a different direction, it's true, but even then, you were still *publishing*. Your *impact* on the culture was probably greater, if perhaps not as easily 'measured,' as readily 'factored.' Yes, in the race to 'publish or perish!,' you *published*. Then, somehow, also perished. Can you tell the court, in your own words, what went wrong?"

I can and most certainly will.

Stirrings in the gallery. Pens at the ready. This is the part we've been waiting for.

Ours is an American tale, a story of random success and hard-won failure. The riches-to-rags journey of a humble idea that became an online article, that became a surprise sensation, that became an editor's interest, that became a manuscript, that became a book. A book that was published and went out into the world, where it was met by silence. Crickets. *The misery of being exploited by capitalists is nothing compared to the misery of not being exploited at all*, said Joan Robinson, and I suspect this was what she meant. She meant the only thing worse than critics are crickets, while the only thing worse than crickets, which I suppose by the transitive property would

personal than a scholar would typically write, but I didn't care, I didn't second-guess it, because I didn't think anyone was paying attention or ever would. It was ostensibly about Keynes, but as I wrote, it became more about myself, about what I have always found interesting in Keynes, and how those things have tended not to be what history or society has found interesting about him. Which then led me, in the article, to consider what that says about me and the field I've chosen, or about my relationship to the world I come from, my innate antagonism toward the culture's way of seeing things, which is weird because of course this is the same culture that made me what I am. What does it say about a culture that it churns out citizens full of antagonism toward itself? It says, "freedom of thought," of course, but it also says a lot of other things. This was before Trump, back when people could still write on topics other than Trump. I wrote about myself and the culture, about being a part of society versus standing apart from it, how skepticism is not indifference but its opposite, Burke's *comic corrective*, Baldwin's *being alone*, a bunch of other stuff. I went wherever my brain took me, then sort of flimsily looped it back to what the culture's done to Keynes, as if I'd planned that all along. I mean, if I had to say what the article was actually *about*—which I did, when the editor who published it didn't like my title and asked for other suggestions—it was finally about optimism. Optimism as a form of antagonism. Thinking as a model for living. In truth, it wasn't a very good article. Or maybe it was: I go back and forth about it. The online magazine that published it was popular but not peer-reviewed, so I knew it wouldn't count for much, career-wise. But so what. My academic work was ahead of schedule. I would get back to my professionally sanctioned Tier 2 scholarship soon enough. In the meantime, I would publish *this*, whatever it was. It would go online, I'd send the link to a few old grad school friends, and that would be it.

"What you did not know," here Keynes steps in, "what you never would have guessed—because how could you?—was that this messy little heartfelt essay would go 'viral,' in the way online articles occasionally do for no apparent reason. Not cat-video viral, but *viral enough* that an editor at a mid-sized university press contacted you. They were launching a series of small non-specialist books, written by scholars but for non-scholarly readers, and he asked if you wanted to turn your article into a book for his series. That must have felt validating."

Very.

"After all, you had not always followed the prescribed path. Since undergrad and particularly through grad school, you prided yourself on your renegade inclinations; not only were you a *feminist* economist but, in your polymathic interests, your tendency to look outside the accepted sources and topics, your refusal to stay within the intellectual confines of the discipline or to wed yourself to the cult of metrics, you had positioned yourself as an outsider in other ways as well. You had taken the road less traveled, and while chasing after tenure had forced you to compromise some of that renegade energy, had threatened to normalize your spirit in ways that worried you, here, by a twist of fate, you had the chance to prove to yourself that you were, in fact, the person you'd always planned and hoped to be. You would write a book. You would put yourself, your thoughts, into the world in the form of a professionally printed, purchasable, publicly available book. You would frame it as a response to one of your favorite essays, 'Economic Possibilities for Our Grandchildren,' then would incorporate the rest of your ideas from there. It would flow out of you easily, just as the article had flowed, like blood from an open vein. It would take . . . six months? Six months at the very most. Hardly a hiccup in the tenure schedule. But it did not take six months."

No.

"In fact, you struggled quite a lot, trying to turn that article into a book."

Yes.

"We needn't go into all the reasons—"

No.

"—since the point is that you finished it. Despite the challenge of raising a child and dealing with an unsupportive department, and despite the various creative and emotional stumbling blocks you met with along the way, you did finish and publish your book within the allotted timeframe of your tenure clock, even if it meant you were unable to write and publish additional peer-reviewed articles during that time."

Keynes stops. He steps to the table on my left, the prosecution's table, and takes a drink from a water glass set there.

He has a settled expression, though it's unclear whether he is allowing the story-so-far to sink in or is mentally gathering himself for revelations yet to come.

Ed said: *Maybe we won't have to move?* But how could we possibly stay? *Those that don't know how to be pros get evicted.* Said Queen Latifah. It's not just a question of money, though his adjunct salary is *not* going to cut it. It's that one way or another, one or the other of us is going to have to find a new job, a raise-a-family sort of job, a *position*, which means either becoming something new, launching into some entirely different profession, preferably one that pays well and requires no particular skills or enthusiasm, or else—at best—means lingering on as a less impressive version of the academic outlier I already am, but in a new town, a new life, a situation much less promising. A position with no future, at a school no one's heard of, with a teaching load twice as large. A one-way dead-end move to a town with nothing for Ed to do and far fewer opportunities for Ali. No history museums or art galleries or science centers, just weedy soccer fields out past the public pool. Just a Cineplex with twelve screens showing the same three movies, a strip of fast-food drive-thrus and car dealerships, and a high school that looks like it was designed in the 1960s by a notorious architect of prisons. The town's population will be almost entirely white, with a range of business-conservative, rural-conservative, and suburban-liberal values, but with zero interest in activism or public debate. A deeply homogenous town. A willfully insular town. Worst of all, there will be nothing to suggest to a curious promising young person like Ali that the world outside might be more interesting or varied or in any way different from the town itself. It will be exactly like where I grew up.

But now Keynes's expression has grown more intent, with a simmering glint in his eye. What is he up to? He puts down the water glass and picks up another object, a sad small item that lay unnoticed on the table this whole time. He holds it up for all to see. It is my book.

"Was it the perfect book she had imagined in her head when she first set out to write it? Of course not. No real book ever manages to live up to the original vision in one's head. Was it a reasonable approximation of the groundbreaking work she'd hoped she would someday write? Perhaps not that either. But was it *tenure*-able? That is all that matters here today, and the answer," announces Keynes, "is, unequivocally, *yes*."

"Perhaps not *in itself*," he qualifies, "no one is saying this book was tenurable *in itself*, but in combination with her considerable scholarly portfolio? I submit exhibit A," he swings my book toward the audience, toward the judge, toward my colleagues, "which is also exhibits B, C, D, all the way to Z. I submit, ladies and gentlemen, that by any metric that gives weight to creativity and curiosity, to the actual work of the mind as opposed to mere mindless adherence to university tenure guidelines, the answer is, irrefutably, yes! And since my client had already, prior to embarking upon this book, quite sufficiently demonstrated her ability to churn out Tier 2 academic papers on a schedule, therefore the only reasonable response by her tenure committee to her ambition to go *beyond* those papers and those guidelines would be *unqualified enthusiasm and support*. Is that how the book was received by your colleagues, with unqualified enthusiasm and support?"

Obviously not.

"But the question is why!" Keynes shouts, suddenly slamming the book to the table, surprising everyone.

"Because there were so few reviews? Surely that is the fault of the publisher as much as the author. Because you were writing on original subjects in an original way? It's no secret that the academy has a vexed relationship with novelty, always preferring to re-tread existing critical paths rather than blaze new ones. But the *real* reason, ladies and gentlemen, or at least the only *specific* reason given by the committee chair—and then only after my client had cornered him in the hallway and made him feel extremely uncomfortable—was the letters! The *outside assessments*."

Instantly, a burst of objections from the defendants.

"Oh, I know we are not supposed to talk about *those*," Keynes shouts over the objections, "*those* are supposed to be held confidential, and it's true that I do not have copies to submit as evidence here today! But it was *cited*, Your Honor. It was the only tangible item clearly if unofficially named by the defendants in denying the plaintiff tenure, and it raises a very interesting question, a terribly important question for us and for academics everywhere: *Should one negative letter be grounds for derailing a career?* Not even a whole letter, it took just a single word, a seemingly judicious but in truth insidious word, a word whose menace hides behind lilting iambs and calming soft vowels, but that nonetheless pummels the heart every time it is uttered. *Derivative*."

God, I hate that word.

"Derivative!"

There's no need to repeat it.

"The absurd thing, of course, being that my client had not even known of Deirdre McCloskey's work until *after* she'd published that original article, had you?"

It wasn't an area I'd been working on, no.

"Not until long after you'd developed your own thoughts along similar though *not at all identical* lines. You hadn't even heard of Professor McCloskey, let alone 'fallen into' her 'camp,' let alone 'leaned too heavily upon' her 'position,' as the confidential assessment unavailable here for evidence purportedly claims. And while of course you did subsequently read Professor McCloskey's work on the rhetoric of economics, since it would have been entirely irresponsible not to, and while you admit it did seem somewhat remarkable that you both had come to a number of overlapping conclusions, and while you further admit finding her work useful, though no more useful than the work of many other unconventional economists, and in fact you ended up feeling that Professor McCloskey might have been more useful had you encountered her earlier, that by the time you came to her work you'd already read too much—you'd read Wayne Booth, for example, and couldn't help feeling that Professor McCloskey had effectively taken Booth's literary and ethical arguments and applied them to economics, which: big deal! I mean, yes, obviously the work Professor McCloskey has done is a *big deal*, her long career has been marked by brilliant achievements, but in terms of your *intellectual overlap*, did it not basically boil down to the fact that you'd both read Wayne Booth? Not exactly a 'camp'! She's not even a Keynesian, your economics are totally different, it's just that you're both interested in these other things, these conceptual things, and you both believe that conceptual things matter. But your ideas push beyond economics and rhetoric. *Your* argument is that, in its finest expressions, in its *potential*, economics is also *utopian*, which is not the same 'camp,' it is not even in the same state, you would have to drive for hours to get from one camp to the other. It is just totally, completely a different argument.

"Which means the writer of that letter, the de-recommender, whose words were used to sink your career, clearly did not read your work closely enough. In fact, knowing, as we do, since it is the general practice in the tenure process, that this letter would have been solicited by the very same group seated here before you, that the de-recommender would have been handpicked by them as someone who shared their views and their values, their smugness, their prejudice, is there not every reason to believe that he—and I think we can all agree

"That you are personally not bound by your institution's metrics and expectations for tenure, for example, simply because you find them archaic? That you are not fully aware that tenure assessments are at the discretion of the tenured faculty and require no explanation at all? Or that in embarking upon an unsanctioned book project, you were taking obvious risks with both your publication record and your time? That you hold no responsibility for the quality or the critical reception of that book? That you in no way allowed your own conflicted feelings about what sort of book it ought to be clutter the clarity of the book's argument? That you were perhaps not actually ready to write that book, which, unlike the scholarly articles you'd written, forced you to manufacture a more personal speaker, a 'self' in language, that would represent you, yourself, to the world? That you never managed to regain, in writing that book, the earnest confidence of the original article, from back when you thought your audience was only a few friends and you didn't constantly second-guess your rhetorical 'pose'? That for too long you'd held in your head many self-romanticizing notions about your position as an outsider, notions that allowed you to feel sure of yourself and important to yourself as long as you were never forced to share them—the notions—with anyone else? That as long as you didn't share this side of yourself with anyone else, it was all unadulterated potential, never forced to perform, never exposed to judgment. That some glimmer of this 'self' had materialized long enough to write that article but this self was not really *you*, it didn't sufficiently encompass *what you care about* or *what you want to say*. Because at the end of the day, you are uniquely ill-equipped to convey to the world *what you care about* or *what you want to say*. You know these things in your mind, or think you know them, and you are capable of saying these things or writing them, but the moment you do, you immediately doubt them. You are capable of being many selves but the moment you commit to one, it becomes an imposter, a dummy to dress up and roll out into the world in your place. And you hate the dummy, hate everything it says, even though it only says what you give it to say, and even though the words you give it to say are the best you can come up with. Which means, must mean, that the fault is not with the dummy but with you. That you are not as brilliant as you've always wanted to believe. As you've needed to believe. That it is easy to be impressed with yourself in private but another thing entirely to project a public self into the world—that this is a skill they don't teach in school, yet so so *so* many people seem to have learned it. How did all these people, effortless at parties, easy on social media, how did they learn to be public? There must have been a moment, an afternoon in elementary school, when an imposing gray eminence showed up to class and passed out everyone's public personas while you were in the bathroom. And here you are decades later still forced to pretend you'd been in class that day, that like everyone else you received your persona, that you've displayed it proudly on your wall ever since. Perhaps the real revelation today is or at least they are better at hiding it. You're better at hiding than at hiding it, better at avoiding than bearing it, better at hoping it will all go away if you lie still eyes closed hands clenched hands clenched *breathe—*

Breathe.

Breathe.

Well, that was awful.

"Yes, sorry about that."

I thought you were *my* lawyer, Keynes.

"Your lawyer, your confidante, your companion on this long night's journey through the house inside your head. But actually, as you know perfectly well, I am just your imagination. Anything I ask, you are asking yourself."

That's even worse.

"Is it? It means you are not really on trial. No one in reality is blaming you for anything. Your family is not blaming you. I, who am dead, am certainly not blaming you. And disappointing as it may be, even your colleagues are no longer thinking about you at all. Only you are blaming you. Only you are questioning your legitimacy, placing yourself in this witness box ostensibly to tell your side of things, to grant yourself justice, if only in your mind. The trouble being that it's here, in your imagination, the place where you ought to feel most safe and free, that you are in fact most weighed down by doubt and fear. Part of you clearly thinks they are *right* about you, even though they can't be, they have to be wrong or else your life's work is pointless, and that is a level of personal negation you cannot possibly survive. No, there's no room for that, no good it would do. Yet it's precisely this fear that leads your imagination to turn your very real problems into this comic inquest, this vaudeville legal proceeding, a chance to slapstick the bad guys while pretending none of it matters very much."

So that's where this court scene came from.

"As a matter of fact, I think it came from children's books. Earlier you were thinking about *Alice in Wonderland* and *The Wind in the Willows*. They both have courtroom scenes."

That's true. I wonder why.

"Perhaps because courtrooms in reality are so adult and boring and horrible, the place where all the worst things end up. The messiness of life organized into categories and assigned consequences. Perhaps it's fear of messiness that leads adults to courtrooms in the first place. Perhaps it's fear of consequences that causes children to enjoy being silly about them in books. Do you suppose you are more like an adult or a child, in this respect?"

I don't even know what I am talking about.

4

It must be after two by now. Maybe it's after three. Maybe it's not even midnight. I would have to sit up to see, and does it really matter? Ali breathing. Ed breathing. Eventually, the morning will come. This night is just a chunk of time that will soon be over and, when it's over, will instantly be forgotten. It may feel like I have arrived at an important moment in my life, but that is just a feeling. It may seem as if various terrible things stored up inside me have chosen tonight to burst forth, but nothing has been stored up inside me. It's all right here all the time. It may feel like there is a *before*, which ended when we all went to bed, and an *after*, which will start whenever the first daylight creeps in between the curtains. But there isn't a before. There isn't really an after. All of this is just a feeling.

5

You know what I need? I need to describe my kitchen.

"You have a nice kitchen."

I have the *nicest* kitchen, Keynes. Not large, but beautifully refinished, every inch designed to my specifications and paid for with a scarily large chunk of our savings, back when we assumed I'd get tenure. Back when Ed assumed, anyway. Now he says, on the bright side, it will boost the house's resale value.

"That is a terrible bright side."

Yes, it is. Nonetheless, I love my kitchen. I can't help it. The green crackled tile. The smooth gray floor-squares. The underhanging open-faced cabinets the contractor handmade from wood he told us had been shipped from Vermont all the way to Spokane before it was shipped back to us, though why he told us this I have no idea. Was it supposed to make the wood seem more exotic because it was shipped around a lot? Or were we supposed to think all that shipping constituted some extra effort on his part? Maybe he was trying to make us feel bad about polluting the environment with all that shipping, because he really didn't want to have to build those cabinets. I had to insist. But then he was very proud of them once they were done. I remember Ed saying that a lot of the pleasure he, Ed, took from the finished cabinets was seeing how proud the contractor was of the job he'd done, the special method he'd used for fitting the sides together and so on, and how he, the contractor, wouldn't have done that work or felt that satisfaction if I hadn't pushed him. Probably Ed said that in response to my asking if I'd been too pushy. That seems like the sort of question I would ask and the sort of answer Ed would give me.

White upper cabinets we picked out at the cabinet store. Chrome pulls we picked out after way too many visits to the pulls store. The revelation that in Late Capitalism we have entire stores that sell nothing but pulls for cabinets and drawers.

I mean it isn't *entirely* fancy. We kept the old stove and refrigerator because they weren't that old and worked fine. We kept the old windows, which are *very* old, because they're beautiful. In fact, when I think about the kitchen, when I put myself inside it and inhabit the feeling of being in that room, which I'm doing now as part of an ancient rhetorical method for remembering speeches, but which also seems to calm me down—what's really most memorable isn't the fancy kitchen it ended up being, but the history that was hidden under the ugly kitchen we'd had before. The hidden house we discovered along the way. *Four* different layers of linoleum, because previous owners had just added a new layer without bothering to pull up the old ones. Those ancient electrical cords they found hanging in the walls, like something Thomas Edison had personally installed. Most amazingly, the hidden window behind the old cabinet on the west wall, which I suppose we knew about ahead of time, since it's right there on the outside of the house, but still, when they actually uncovered it, when they knocked out the cabinet and it let light into the house for the first time in who knows how long—*that* was exciting. Like digging up treasure. And it opened just fine!

Then studying the floor beneath the hidden window, the real wood floor at last unburdened of all that linoleum, they figured out that the window had not originally been part of the kitchen at all, but that this little section had once been a powder room, probably opening onto the dining room rather than the kitchen. Which explained the hidden window's frosted glass. But it turned out that *that* wall, the section of the west wall where the powder room had been, wasn't quite flush with the rest of that side of the kitchen, it was a little pushed out from the rest—since it had once been a different room—which meant that in order to hang the new cabinets and put in the new counter they had to strip the whole wall down to brick and build a two-by-two wood frame over it. Which was a smart solution, I thought, all things considered. Our contractors were smart guys. Also funny—I liked them. We all did. Thank goodness, too, since they were there almost every day for *weeks*. They would show up in the morning in their work boots with their thermoses and it was like having friends over, old funny friends. Old funny friends who redo your kitchen.

One day while they were working, while Ed was out mowing, two old ladies pulled up outside. I heard Ed talking to someone and saw a black SUV at the curb, then he called me out to introduce me. Two laughing sisters who'd lived in the house as children, forty or fifty years ago, in town for a family reunion. We couldn't invite them in, because the construction guys had their gear everywhere, so they sat in their car while we talked and talked. They had stories about everything. We figured out how various features had changed since they'd lived there, a closet where a door used to be, the coal chute in the basement. At some point the sister in the driver's seat said, "Is the combination to the wall safe still . . ." then rattled off three numbers, and Ed instantly freaked out. He'd been trying to crack that little round wall safe since we'd moved in. Ali had decided it was filled with either jewelry or a treasure map or skeletal remains. So the sister in the passenger seat pulled out a scrap of paper and the other sister wrote down the combination she still remembered after forty or fifty years, all of us laughing the whole time, because who could believe it? But sure enough, later when Ed tried it out: voilà! The only thing inside was a note with the safe's combination, probably left by the previous owner and accidentally locked in there by the real estate agent, but still, it was exciting.

And all of this, the people, the whole process made me aware of our house in an entirely different way. Of how really old it was, how many lifetimes had been lived there. So I ended up loving my kitchen not just for how nice it is *now*, but because in fixing it up, in digging out all the nasty linoleum and freeing the hidden window and dealing with the weird old pipes the plumber found in the basement ceiling, through all of that I grew to care about the house more. The antipathy I'd felt toward the ugly kitchen we'd originally moved into was replaced by respect for the many kitchens it had previously been. I developed an uncharacteristically sentimental, borderline gushy feeling that in fixing it up I had done something *nice* for the kitchen, something *caring* for the kitchen, and that we were all in it together now, this journey of life, just me and Ed and the kitchen. The years would pass and we would look out for each other. We would cook countless meals together, bake holiday cakes and pies together, see Ali off to college, grandkids would one day run in and out from the dining room—*Slow down! Slow down!*—and through it all the kitchen would remain not only beautiful but happy. A happy kitchen. A well-cared-for kitchen. Which has now been reduced to its resale value.

Are you really going to mourn your kitchen? *That's* what you're going to mourn?

One upside to living in the apocalypse is that it puts your problems into perspective.

It's not just a kitchen, though. The kitchen is metonymic.

And also, yes, I am allowed to mourn my kitchen.

If these days most economists tend to dismiss "Economic Possibilities for Our Grandchildren" as either frivolous or deeply flawed, this is because they suffer from what I would call a *failure of imagination*. They think the sole purpose of writing is to convey information, and they refuse to acknowledge that any effort at writing, even the driest assemblage of mathematical models and stilted prose, has not only logical and informative aspects but also aspects of performance and persuasion, and therefore its purpose is not limited only to the facts and figures it conveys. There is, in other words, a *rhetorical* side to economics. *Rhetorical* not in the sense of a question that you're not supposed to answer, but in the sense of belonging to the art of rhetoric, an art that economists, like most people, tend to look down upon—"That's all just rhetoric!"—as if rhetoric is some horrible thing.

Rhetoric is not a horrible thing, ladies and gentlemen, though it does have one of the longest-running bad reputations in all of human history. People have been pooh-poohing rhetoric since Plato called it "the art of clever speeches," and even earlier, from the origins of democracy itself. For they were born together, democracy and rhetoric. They were invented at the same time, by the same person, a guy named Cleisthenes. I mean, he didn't *invent* them, but that's where Western history marks the spot. The irony being that we think of democracy as this very *good* thing, the embodiment of freedom and equality, while conveniently forgetting that rhetoric—the shaping of public opinion—which we're quick to call a *bad* thing, is the only way democracy actually works. It was the birth of democracy that turned speech-making into a career, and the original careerists of democratic speech-making were called the Sophists, from which term we derive the word "sophistry," which is even more universally maligned than "rhetoric." It means, or has come to mean, manipulative, deceptive language. "Clever speeches." It's a slur built right into the English language, like "shysters" but without the racist overtones.

Whereas the ancient Greeks preferred to treat their Sophists *with* the racist overtones, because you see the original Sophists were not native Athenians but itinerant scholars, foreigners—a fact often overlooked, but very much worth bearing in mind. Unlike most Athenians, the Sophists had traveled the world. They knew that Athenian ideas of truth and virtue were different from the ideas of truth and virtue in other places, and this knowledge, this understanding that the Athenian way was not the only way, that cultural truths were relative and contingent, this intellectual open-mindedness was deeply annoying to dogmatic xenophobic Athenians, like Plato, who was a total elitist, by the way, and hated democracy, because he thought average people were too dumb to make their own decisions and ought to be governed by philosophers, because philosophers alone understand "essential truths." Apparently he never met anyone from our philosophy department. But is it any wonder, then, that Plato hated the Sophists, who taught that truth was specific to each situation and determined through language and argument rather than inherited from the gods?

Not that the Sophists were perfect. They didn't always help their own case. It didn't help that they got filthy rich off their lessons, for example, and at least one of them—Gorgias—advertised that his speeches could convince anyone to believe anything, which is not exactly the sort of claim that builds trust.

Incidentally, if any of you are interested, you should look up the ancient *female* rhetorician Aspasia from Miletus, who was a contemporary of Gorgias, but is much, much more interesting. She was partner to the statesman Pericles—not concubine, *partner*—and a teacher to Socrates, Plato's own beloved teacher, at a time when such roles for women simply did not exist. Evidence suggests it was actually Aspasia who invented the method of argumentation-by-questioning that became known to history as the Socratic method, that bedrock chestnut of the patriarchal Western intellectual tradition. Behind every great man, there's a great woman's rhetorical method. Unfortunately, none of Aspasia's own writing survived, so we are stuck with what men said about her. History being whatever the say-ers say, of course. Of course of course. A horse is a horse. Where was I.

Rhetoric got a bad reputation via the Sophists, for legitimate and less legitimate reasons, which led a Sophist named Isocrates to introduce a moral grounding to their relativism by tying rhetoric to the ideals of wisdom and pragmatism: even though we could not actually know *the truth* about anything, still a *kind of* truth could be arrived at by considering all the available opinions, and a wise rhetorician was someone who weighed all the information in order to make decisions that were *more or less* the best available. I think of this as the birth of pragmatism in the Western intellectual tradition. Unfortunately, it did little to curb rhetoric's feud with the philosophers. Plato's protégé, Aristotle, thought Isocrates was full of crap. He zings him: "Just because most people *don't* act rationally doesn't mean they *shouldn't* or don't *need to*." Isocrates zings back: "I'd rather form reasonable opinions about useful things than claim precise knowledge of things that are totally useless." Is it better to be right or to be useful?

That is an argument philosophy and rhetoric have been having ever since.

And no, before you ask, I do not think that all of this belongs in my talk tomorrow, or even most of it, though I'll want to include at least the part about Cleisthenes, and how rhetoric and democracy go hand in hand. But the point to most of the rest is simply that I am *enjoying* myself thinking about all of this: the history of rhetoric, the history of ideas. Feminist heroines and patriarchal feuds. It's all so much simpler, so much more stimulating and less exhausting than having to revisit, re-digest, and restructure in my mind the argument of a book I hate thinking about and sometimes regret having written. In fact, I wish I could just switch topics tomorrow without telling anyone and spend the whole time talking about the history of rhetoric instead.

Actually.

I mean, what's the worst they could do?

Of the Sophists, it's Isocrates who becomes the important figure down the line. While Aristotle at this point gets forgotten for centuries, Isocrates is a major influence on all the Roman rhetoricians, like Cicero and Quintilian, who build on his idea of "wisdom" to propose a rhetoric centered on the *orator perfectus*, or *vir bonus dicendi peritus*, the good person who speaks well. The basic idea being that speaking well is a form of goodness, and that to speak well and eloquently you don't need "essential truths," but you do have to be a good person and care about the right things. There's a kind of optimism built into this, as well as a hometown conservatism, the assumption that Roman values were the right values, perhaps more so for Quintilian than for Cicero, since Quintilian ended up rich while Cicero ended up with his severed head hung in the middle of Rome. But aside from *that*, there's also an *optimism*, the belief that people are essentially good—however you define "good"—and therefore only goodness will persuade them. Good will out! This optimism then becoming, in turn, a model for much of what we think of as the Western liberal mindset. It inspired us in the early days of Obama, then depressed us when Republicans walked all over him. And it's the attitude John Maynard Keynes adopts in "Economic Possibilities for Our Grandchildren," if in fact I stick to the original plan tomorrow and need to connect this Rhetoric portion of my speech—still here in the kitchen!—back to the subject overall.

That subject being *economists* and how, in wanting to believe that the work they are doing is "scientific," aimed at truth by establishing facts and proofs *rather than* an ongoing negotiation of provisional truths through persuasion—in failing, in other words, to recognize, or at least to emphasize, the narrative and rhetorical context in which their writing and modeling take place, or the basic fact that they are effectively, inescapably, *telling stories*—a point that the very smart and interesting economist Deirdre McCloskey made back in the early '90s, but which I also arrived at *entirely on my own*, though unfortunately much later, because none of my professors or advisors ever mentioned McCloskey to me, either because they'd never read her work or for some reason thought I wouldn't need to—but the—what was I saying? Why economists, failing to understand the rhetorical nature of their work, therefore have also misunderstood Keynes's "Economic Possibilities for Our Grandchildren," along with the entire way of thinking about *rhetorical purpose* that his essay implies. And a corollary question, which has been hovering in the background this whole time, which I've mostly been blowing past but suddenly find myself needing to answer, as I listen to myself go on and on, which is how anyone attending this talk tomorrow could possibly care about any of this.

Keynes?

"Yes?"

You're still here.

"Behind you. Beside the refrigerator."

Can you tell me why anyone would attend this talk tomorrow?

"Curiosity, I suppose. Intellectual stimulation."

I am having trouble imagining why someone would want to venture out in the middle of the day, in the middle of the workweek, to sit in an auditorium and watch me talk about these things.

"Entertainment? Edification? Personal growth?"

I mean, who *are* these people?

"I . . . hm."

Don't they have anything better to do?

Keynes?

"Yes."

I've just had what may turn out to be the most depressing thought of the entire night.

"Oh dear."

I don't even want to form this thought out loud in my head.

"Yet I feel confident that you almost certainly will."

What if *this* is the future your essay was predicting, where no one has to work so instead they spend their days sitting in auditoriums watching failed academics present their untenured theories on optimism?

Keynes?

"Still here."

Does the situation of my being a failed academic with an inconsequential book and a bleak future speaking tomorrow to a room full of people with nothing better to do resemble, in any way, the future you predicted? Because it does not resemble the future that I predicted for myself.

"Which was what?"

Exactly.

"You mean you don't know?"

I mean I never quite spelled it out for myself.

"Perhaps that was the problem."

At least I don't remember doing so. I have a terrible memory when it comes to my own life, particularly when it comes to large existential abstract questions like "What did you think your life would be, back when you were young and were thinking ahead to the person you would be now?" Mostly my younger self just followed her instincts, I think. Followed instincts and latched on to whatever opportunities presented themselves. Looking back, it's easy to pretend that I chose the path that led here, but I know it was more passive than that. I didn't lack courage, but what I really had was a sort of faith in the future that resembled, more than anything, a total absence of strategy. I was ready to be steered. It wasn't books or ideas that steered me, though. It wasn't goals and plans. It wasn't anything I discovered on my own that brought me here. It was people who I met at different times in different places. I won't say at the *right* or *wrong* times, just times. Maggie. Evelyn. Even Ed, in his way. And it was something about me, too, of course. The oddities of who I am. The person I've been, if not always, then from very far back. It was that wandering Abby with her peculiar predilections occasionally stumbling upon someone who showed her what it was like to live with purpose. It was people with purpose, or with what looked to me like purpose, providing models of how to meaningfully exist in this world. I suppose *that* was the future I pictured for myself: meaningful presence.

Somehow, someday, I would become *myself* for the world, and someday, somehow, that would matter.

"Well," says Keynes, "to answer your original question regarding how economists have tended to take my predictions, in case you want to wrap that up before heading too far in this new self-reflective and potentially very depressing direction, I believe a large part of your original point was that I was not earnestly *predicting* anything at all."

Keynes, who did not believe economists could know the future, or else they'd all be filthy rich. Who speculated in the stock market, yes, but often lost. Who—more importantly— saw economics as a perpetual work in progress, its purposes not Platonic, not dealing with "essential truths," but rather Isocratic, seeking "reasonable opinions about useful things." For whom economics was a place to try things out, to risk and fail. Whose own thinking was always evolving, and who, when charged with inconsistency, quipped, "When I get new evidence I change my mind. What do you do?" Keynes whose most famous idea was that governments should use policy and investment to solve short-run problems instead of waiting for free markets to fix them in the long run. Whose most famous quote was "In the long run, we are all dead." Who said, less famously, though I have a sticky note of it stuck to the wall in my office, "There is no reason why we should not feel ourselves free to be bold, to be open, to experiment, to take action, to try the possibilities of things." Does anyone seriously think *this* man, who had no children or grandchildren but was deeply invested in improving people's lives here and now, wrote "Economic Possibilities for Our Grandchildren" because he was really concerned with what the world would look like in a hundred years?

So what was he up to, then?

The answer to that, ladies and gentlemen, currently awaits us in my office.

Which is upstairs.

6

Probably it's a blessing, my terrible memory. The past is filled with moments I am happy to forget.

History is the nightmare from which I am trying to awake. Those are the sorts of memories that come easily. Unbidden. Random quotes from famous people.

The barrier between oneself and one's knowledge of oneself is high indeed.

The difference between who you are and all the junk you've packed into your head.

* * *

There are times, though, when I do wish my memory was better. For example, right now. I have been calm, or calmish, for a while now. Or anyway I've been calm *enough*, and for long enough, that I would say I am doing very well. In fact, I am feeling existentially attuned, lying here in the dark, mulling it all over, and my natural inclination is to look back on things, the past. To trace a storyline through the past in order to explain to myself how I've ended up where I am.

Here, in this life.

Here, in this profession. This predicament.

In this family.

This self, this "personality."

In this city, this hotel room, this bed, this head.

Climbing the stairs of the imaginary house in this head, noticing, as I might in my actual house, that this stairwell holds almost no memories. Several times Ed has asked about hanging pictures along the walls here. Left to his own devices, he would almost certainly install one of those stepped galleries of family portraits and vacation photos that have long been the exclusive province of home stairwells, like in my own house growing up. But I have always stopped that idea in its tracks, saying simply and truthfully that it seems pretty kitschy to me. That I prefer my own stairwell empty, thank you. A quick uncarpeted seven steps up to a clutter-free landing, a brisk turn to another seven steps, and all around you the walls are high and blank and smooth, utterly free of the marks of identity. A corridor of clean slates.

Your memory is not as bad as you think, though. No Keynes this time, just me. *Your memory is not as bad as you'd* like to *think.*

Is that true?

You just choose not to use it.

Maybe that's true.

Maggie changed my life but it was Evelyn who led me to Maggie.

Or, it was Evelyn who took me from being someone who might not have found Maggie, might never have noticed what was so wonderful about Maggie, and turned me into someone who could and did.

Do I really want to think about Evelyn?

A white dog lies dead on the floor of a black basement.

Think about Maggie instead.

Because I'd been Evelyn's friend for a while, by then. Because I admired her and had come, through her, to be interested in "experimental music" and "experimental art," the word "experimental" and the lifestyle it promised. More life*style*, at that point—new to me, but also a natural extension of the person I'd always been, of the various forms of expression I'd tried on over the years. My classical period. My year and a half of hip-hop. My indie rock minute. All of it exciting but none of it sticking, not that sticking was even a goal. Permanently defining myself was never a goal. More like *not* defining myself, always changing. "Experimental." Because despite all of that, and despite all the new ideas I'd gotten into through Evelyn, I was still, in my classes and by official declaration, majoring in economics.

It was like living a double life, the only econ student at the punk shows and art openings. Like Keynes and his Bloomsbury group, though I wouldn't have made that connection back then. *Back then* Keynes wasn't a real person to me at all, not an actual human with a life and ideas but just an irritating adjective on the blackboard: *Keynesian, Keynesian, Keynesian.* It meant a universe I wasn't yet a part of, and wasn't sure I wanted to be. Experimental art and music were urgent and exciting, even for someone with no talent, while economics, which I was actually good at, was rigid, institutional, male-dominated, and in general pretty dull.

Until one day, sifting through course offerings for the coming semester, I stopped on "Experimental Economics," a onetime class by a visiting—female!—professor. It was as random as that. It was the word "experimental" and the momentary thrill it gave me that the two worlds I'd been straddling might meaningfully overlap. Was I disappointed to find out this "experimental" meant something totally different? Maybe for the first five minutes. Not after listening to Maggie, though. Not after watching Maggie model for a roomful of students how to be a mature human being full of curiosity and intelligence. It meant clinical studies, data collection. Designing experiments to study how people make choices. Okay. It didn't mean avant-garde theories or the rejection of the status quo, but there was still a spirit of newness to it. It wasn't what everyone else was doing. Not that I ended up developing any great passion for experimental economics that semester, but so what. That class was about Maggie. It was Maggie 101.

She didn't use notes but would stand in the middle of the room and ask simple questions as if they'd just come into her head. What questions? A lot of *why*s. Why do you think that? Why does that matter? Like a grown-up version of Ali age three. Why this? Why that? Brain like a vacuum cleaner. Driving her around in the car, listening to her voice broadcast out from the back seat: *Why? Why?* Having to rethink and explain from scratch the simplest elements of everyday life. Which was Maggie, too, but for our benefit rather than hers. The best teacher I ever had asked the questions of a three-year-old. *Why? Why?* Because she wanted us to wonder, is why. Because undergraduates are all so *used to* everything.

"Not very convincing," she wrote in red on the front page of the first paper I handed in. I already idolized her by then, so this was crushing. I spent twice as long on the second paper, but she wrote the same thing. For much of that semester, I almost certainly hated her.

With the final paper, I struggled and struggled. Finally, it came out in a gush of earnestness, much the way, years later, that article about Keynes would come out in a gush of rigorous earnestness. An earnestness and a vulnerability that are obviously parts of me, though I can't always access them when I write. Nor would I *always* want to. Or often, even. Earnest and vulnerable being only two of a million ways to be. I handed in the paper with great seriousness and barely concealed disdain. When she handed it back, the red scrawl said, "This is good writing." Then—what? A chorus of angels sang? Clouds parted? Doves flew? This memory smells funny. Perfumy. It's accurate, it's almost certainly accurate, but it makes Maggie out to be one of those tough-love inspirational teachers from TV. Has my memory turned Maggie into a TV cliché? Or—other option—maybe it was not my memory but my undergraduate imagination that made Maggie an inspirational character. Maybe my memory of her is accurate, but it's a memory of how I experienced her, rather than of who she was. It's who she was *for me*. That seems right. The memories I have of her later, when I'm older, are more mundane. The Maggie I corresponded with through grad school, the Maggie who got divorced, left her career, and moved to New Zealand, is just a woman, a friend.

Angels sang, clouds parted—and I showed up at her office at the end of that fall semester, ostensibly to ask about a course she was offering in the spring.

Since she was only there for the year, they'd put her in that attic office at the very top of the econ building. The room was a floor to itself, a crow's nest, with a low ceiling and with half-circle windows on three sides. It was cozy and lined with boxes she'd never unpacked, a big wooden desk, and those wooden swivel chairs you see in newspaper offices in old movies.

"You probably won't find it very interesting," she said about the spring course. "I'm covering a lot of the same material, just from a slightly different direction."

"That sounds great, actually," I said. "To be honest, I think I'm more interested in the directions we approach subjects from than in the subjects themselves." Did I mean that? It wasn't anything I'd ever said to myself. It just came out of my mouth. "Is that an awful thing to admit?"

"No, of course not," said Maggie. "That's probably true about you," which may have been a compliment, or just as easily a criticism, but in either case was the first indication that she, or any teacher ever, had given particular thought to who I was or what I might be interested in. "But there are always new ways to come at any subject," she went on, "and there are a lot of other subjects that might interest you more. If you'd like, we could do an independent study." None of this said with any great warmth, yet I have never felt more special than I did right then.

"Early Women Economists": not Maggie's specialization, but that was part of the lesson, to be full of curiosity, that a scholar can have a lively mind, can care as much about historical perspectives as about clinical studies as about everything else. That a clinician can tell a whole feminist history, from Dorothy Brady to Margaret Reid, Joan Robinson to Barbara Bergmann, women economists with ideas. Measuring household production. Factoring homemaking into the GNP. The economic value of unpaid work. Advocating consumer protections. Combining econometrics with historical and sociological perspectives. Subjects that made so much sense to me, so instantly, that I wondered why I'd even bothered with economics before that. What interest had economics held for me back before I'd discovered *this*? Women's roles in the economy and the academy. Women's roles in government and policy. Economies are made up of more than just men; economics is made up of more than just math. A larger picture. A less gendered picture. A more inclusive picture. Inclusivity is simply accuracy. Skepticism toward standard methodology. What gets measured and what's left out. Who does the measuring and from what perspective. Rigor without acknowledgment. Innovation without acknowledgment. Male colleagues and their prizes. Permanent income hypothesis. Gender wage gap. Independent thinking. Independent study. Talks in Maggie's office. Walks along the quad. Red scribbles over everything. Occasional encouraging check marks. Later I would find contemporary discourses, non-Anglocentric discourses, living thinkers more radical than any Maggie talked about—the more radical the better—a deeper reading of pedagogical and representational issues, global systems, the sources and varieties of inequity. Later I would see how large the conversation truly was, and would struggle to find my place in it. But there, in Maggie's office, my adulthood was born. Evelyn helped me shake off my overripe youth, but it was Maggie who made me a grown-up.

Maggie and Evelyn. They never even met. I doubt they would have liked each other. Maggie's too pragmatic. Evelyn's too—
No, Evelyn was just Evelyn. She was exactly the right amount.
I am not thinking about Evelyn now, however.

Then there was a period during which Maggie and I were out of touch, after Ed and I entered grad school, or *I* entered and he tagged along, then started grad school himself a year later—because why not?—and ended up finishing before me, but only because he was in a different program, and anyway the whole point is that, for a while there, things were busy. Either things were busy or I just couldn't find a good reason to write to her, nothing particular to ask or say. I was reading *Feminist Economics*, discovering that larger world, and feeling frankly pretty impressed with myself, even if part of me could never stop second-guessing, self-doubting, the perpetual wrench in my personal reinvention. Maybe I needed to stay away from Maggie while I figured some of that out.

Those grad school days were good, though, the days of wine and bike rides, whole mornings reading in bed, or afternoons under a tree, evening lectures, movie marathons, meet up for dinner—somewhere in the midst of which Ed and I planned that road trip to see everybody's babies. The Baby Tour. So many friends were having them, and it seemed important to visit while our lives allowed us time, and while our friends still resembled the people we'd known, before parenthood gobbled them up. We split the driving and covered massive exhausting swaths of America each day. We were adults but young, we were fun, not in any hurry, heading wherever the babies were. The future was coming, but would hold off for a little bit longer. Maggie was nowhere near the babies, but was not far off route on the way to Ed's brother's house, so that was when I saw her again.

We met at her office, because I'd waited to email until we were already on the road, and I guess she needed to be in her office that day. A fairly dull office, I thought, modern, airy, equipped with corporate furniture, nothing like the cozy attic nook where my journey with Maggie had started. She stopped working when I arrived, and we talked for a long time, while Ed wandered around campus. I told her what I'd been reading and thinking, and she was interested, listening, but she didn't have much to say, which surprised me. I thought she'd have a lot to say. Maybe I hoped for advice or direction. A few years later, when she told me she was retiring, it occurred to me that she must have been slowing down for a while by then, looking already toward the next part of her life. Probably she had not been knocking herself out reading all the new things I was reading. But at the time, not knowing that, knowing only that this was Maggie, the person who'd put me on my path, the path I'd since been barreling down without her, it was all a little disappointing. I had the audacity to wonder if I'd outgrown her. When in fact that day turned out to be the start of another stage in our relationship, because as I was leaving, she handed me a copy of Keynes's *Essays in Persuasion* from a pile on her desk. Keynes who I thought I already knew, but whose writing I'd never actually read, an embarrassingly superficial sort of knowledge, though if I'm being honest, that's probably true even now about most of my so-called knowledge of writers I so-called know. "You'd like this," she said, "and I have an extra." Since I had no idea how important that book would become for me, I didn't think much of it at the time. But if I'm counting up formative life moments, obviously that one counts.

When did I stop thinking about the past? Ali's birth? Earlier? You close down that wing of your house to open up another. Yet I seem to recall being practically obsessed with my own past all through my twenties. All through my *teens*. It seems, when I look back on it, that the younger I was, the greater fascination I felt toward the various people I had previously been. Nostalgia. I valued my memories much more, then. Too much.

Maybe the value of memories, as with any other commodity, is a function of scarcity. When you first notice that you have some, you have relatively few, so they seem to matter more. You are fascinated with the fact that you have them at all. Self-awareness. Growing up. But as you begin to accumulate memories with the years, their relative utility diminishes.

You grow into a more realistic appreciation of their worth, then eventually even that dwindles. Finally, there are so many memories, and you are so used to having them around, so accustomed to their plentitude, that your demand curve approaches zero, and your past, your entire personal history, seems hardly worth the effort of remembering at all.

Did I just discover an economic explanation for why young people are self-absorbed? And why old people can't be bothered? Perhaps the Nobel Prize is still on the table.

The last time I saw her she was packing up her office. *Our* office, since she had to move out before I could move in. We'd met for dinner the night before, but I'd decided to stop by unannounced after a morning of faculty orientation, because there were things I should have said at dinner, things I'd meant to say but hadn't. She was wearing workout clothes, those expensive yoga pants that are somehow always slimming, and my first thought was that in all the time I'd known her, I'd never seen her in anything other than suits. Pantsuits, skirt suits. But of course, I thought, she wears other things! A reminder that our relationship had always known very particular parameters. Her role in my life had been monumental, more important than she would ever know, but in most ways, we had never really been close.

She seemed irritated. From our conversation the night before, I gathered she'd had a trying few months. Probably it had been a trying few years, given all she'd gone through. But seeing as she was leaving for New Zealand soon, and this was likely the last time I would see her in person, I'd come to her office hoping for—something warmer than this.

"Anyway," I said, after some chitchat while she riffled through boxes, "this seems a good time to say thank you."

She looked up. "For what?"

"Oh, you know. For everything."

"*Everything?*" As if she didn't understand.

"For helping me get this job, for one."

She smiled. She saw the conversation we were having. Okay.

She didn't say anything, though, and promptly went back to packing. A few beats later she said, "This job," but to herself. As if she were having a conversation with, and about, herself. As if it was *her* job I'd meant, not the exciting new career I'd just embarked upon, but some crinkly old used one she'd found among her boxes. A crinkly old career that I was more than welcome to, if I wanted it, because she wouldn't need it where she was going. It was just going to sit in this box getting moldy anyway.

No "But Abby, you earned this job!"

Something must have happened just before I got there, I decided, standing in the mouth of her office. An irritating exchange with a colleague or frustrating news from the department chair, some last-minute logistical headache she hadn't counted on. I'd caught her at a bad moment. I'd surprised her. It was fine. Rather disappointing that this temporary frustration, whatever it was, could keep her from engaging in any meaningful way with my awkwardly heartfelt expression of gratitude—but oh well. Life happens. We talked a little longer, said some other, less memorable things. I left with the promise that we'd email. Which we have, but not much, and not lately. Maybe not ever again. Maybe it's one of those relationships that die in one-sided awkward silence, with the other side never knowing what went wrong. I doubt she's even heard about my debacle. I doubt news of my professional upheaval has reached faraway New Zealand. Who would have told her other than me? I don't want her to feel responsible, though, and anything I'd say would sound like, *You're not responsible!*, as if she actually is, even though she obviously isn't.

I walked outside and started across campus, sticking to the grassiest and shadiest parts. I'd been there only a few days but had already figured out for myself the shadiest cross-campus route. In fact, I had an outdoor good-weather route *and* an indoor bad-weather route already scouted, one or the other of which I have in fact followed practically every day since. It was late summer and extremely hot, even in the shade. Probably I should have taken the indoor route, but I was feeling surprisingly lively. Light, expansive. I was not dwelling on my disappointing conversation with Maggie, but thinking more generally about careers and what they amount to. What Maggie's career had amounted to. The work she'd done had meant something to the world, and her teaching had meant quite a lot to me personally. But I could already see, from the professional perch I had just recently assumed, looking out across the future of my own burgeoning career and thinking about what it would look like when I myself was retiring—I could see how even a career as productive as Maggie's might look small, in the end, to the person who lived it. I was not depressed, or annoyed at Maggie, but instead was enjoying a kind of pride at how understandable it all seemed. Maggie's feelings. Maggie's situation. Everyone's situation, in the end. How human it was. How inevitable, but also, if you handled it right, if you approached life with the right attitude, how manageable. The toil I'd experienced in my twenties, the struggle with my own fantasies of greatness, *or whatever*, the mental work I'd done to disabuse myself of vague romantic notions of what I would someday accomplish, all of that seemed, in light of this new completely reasonable mindset, to have paid off. I was an adult. I had a career. I understood what Maggie's career amounted to, and I did not need to pretend that I would accomplish more. Or that my end point would be any better. My career would be what it would be. My life was not larger than anyone else's. I felt present, prepared. I even knew enough to know that I could not hang on to this wonderfully enlightened perspective. This was just another attitude I was moving through, and my future self would cycle through all my other moods as regularly as ever.

It did *not* occur to me that within a few years I would gamble my livelihood and my family's future on publishing a small book with a medium-sized university press. Nor that a

7

"What are you supposed to be?"

One recurring nightmare is not enough reason to keep her out of my memory, not here in this sleepless vigil that I rationally know is of no consequence but that *feels* like a final accounting, a cataloging of all things, as if I've arrived at some profound existential destination rather than just a particularly acute bout of hyperactivity for the busy brain trapped in this stationary body, the mommy-mummy, monster to most but unsung hero to her loved ones, a sweet husband-daughter duo who will never know the epic battles she fought, through the darkest hours, so that they could get some sleep.

"What are you supposed to be?" said Evelyn, and I looked up.

* * *

"What are you supposed to be?" meaning my costume, which melded B-movie robot and little Dutch girl, a robotic Dutch girl, with a triangular bonnet made of tinfoil and a crinkly unsexy dress I'd "sewn" by duct-taping loose tinfoil to a disposable basting pan cut into bra cups, all of it held up by tinfoil straps. Evelyn was dressed as a gigolo. Her gorgeous naturally curly Brazilian hair was slicked back and smashed down, and since I didn't know her yet, and since the rest of her costume was so purposefully repulsive—the wiry fake chest hair, the stippled-on beard, the rampant polyester—I could only *sort of* tell how beautiful she was.

"A robotic Dutch girl," I said. "Don't ask me why. It's not like I had a lot of tinfoil and duct tape hanging around already, or a basting pan. It's not like I looked at a drawer full of this stuff and thought, What could I make with that? No, I actually went out and bought it all *in order to be* a robotic Dutch girl."

It was a party and I was already a little drunk.

"You were going for Most Original," she offered.

"They're having a contest?"

"Oh, no. I mean, maybe? Who knows. They should."

I was sitting alone on a couch and she was standing—noncommittally, I thought—beside the chair across from me.

"I didn't want to be just another slutty cat or slutty vampire," I went on. "In high school, everyone was always a slutty cat or vampire. I once tried going as a slutty hamster, but I just looked like Bigfoot. I mean, it had a bra." Why was I talking about high school? This party was filled with interesting people.

"Well, I like it," said Evelyn, and she sat, which was nice. "It's very chaste. Feminine, yet impenetrable."

"That's what I was going for! Approachable imperviousness. You?"

"Biohazardous masculinity." She displayed herself.

"Your chest hair *is* super gross."

"Thanks," she said. "I'm Evelyn."

The time she had free tickets to a concert at the symphony hall but it was not the symphony, it was Ornette Coleman. Loud and frenetic and I didn't like the music at first, but the experience was exciting. Free-form jazz in a fancy hall, the clash of the modern sounds with all the cushiony red velvet. The music I found hard to follow, it lacked shape, or the sort of shape I was used to music having, and I guess Evelyn noticed how I was feeling.

"What I do when I have trouble getting into music," she said between songs, "is I turn it into a finger opera." She held up her fingers and performed a little puppet show, one index finger hopping headlong into the other, less like opera than Punch and Judy. But when the music came back, she was right, doing a little finger skit made the sound open up for me. Which is a very silly way to listen to Ornette Coleman, and I was surprised that someone as cool as Evelyn would suggest it. But it took the pressure off. The pressure to "get it," to figure out what I was "supposed to" think. It was the pressure, more than the music, that was in the way.

"All the famous avant-garde composers are men—not all the composers, just all the *famous* ones—because it's men who write music history, and they write about other men."

I am standing there nodding but inside I'm struck, like a revelation, that the same is true of economics. Why struck? Because music and economics were, or seemed to be, such different worlds. And music was, or up to then had seemed to be, so much cooler.

Evelyn is at a drum kit and I'm behind a marimba holding the mallets in a throat-choking grip that I know, from having seen actual marimba players, isn't even close. She's laying down a rhythm that feels rock-steady at first, like a rhymed couplet, like a stanza of Dr. Seuss, but that occasionally breaks time entirely, as if too much rhythm was accidentally poured into that one particular measure and a few beats of it spilled out on the ground. We're playing. It feels loose. Chaotic, but in control. And we're talking, too, not while we're playing, but whenever we stop.

It's men who write music history, she's saying, and history is just whatever gets written, which is why history always misses so much of what's going on.

Pamela Z sings and records her voice and loops and changes it in real time, recording her voice to immediately accompany herself still singing.

Ellen Fullman plays on strings that stretch across a room, strings so long that if you pluck them the sound is lower than the human ear can hear. She puts on sneakers and walks up and down, running her fingers along their length to make the strings resonate. Walking music. We saw her do it live. No doubt she's out in the world doing it somewhere still.

Laurie Anderson's computerized voice: funny and serious and perplexing and approachable and very '80s sounding.

Charlotte Moorman playing cello in a bra made out of little TV sets.

Cathy Berberian.

Diamanda Galás.

Music as performance art.

In the arty "performance art" sense of performance art. Obviously, music is a performance art.

John Cage's essays and lectures were exciting to read, while his compositions were half the time hauntingly beautiful and the other half just sort of meh.

Björk I'd listened to in high school. Björk I already loved.

Pauline Oliveros is probably the most famous twentieth-century avant-garde woman composer, though I personally preferred listening to that French woman whose name I'm not remembering, but whose music sounded, to me anyway, very similar, but a little bit better.

Evelyn explaining Oliveros's concept of "deep listening," which she was reading about at the time.

Me wondering out loud whether the reason Oliveros was more famous than the French composer I liked so much was because Oliveros coined this term, "deep listening," and the most famous person in any situation is whoever coins a term.

Evelyn taking this question to mean that I wasn't that interested in Oliveros or "deep listening," which wasn't at all what I was saying. Either she'd misread my whimsy, or else I'd struck a nerve. That happened sometimes. For all her generosity of spirit, she also had nerves, and I was occasionally surprised by what struck them.

Women in labs composing on tape reels.

Daphne Oram.

Laurie Spiegel.

Ambient, minimalist, electronic.

Delia Derbyshire at the BBC Radiophonic Workshop. She wrote the theme to *Doctor Who*, as well as a lot of other electronic music just about as creepy sounding as the theme to *Doctor Who*.

Mary Jane Leach.

Annea Lockwood.

Once I get started, it all flows out.

Alice Coltrane, especially those recordings that are just bass and harp. The incredible variety of musical experiences that can be created with just a bass and a harp.

And Christina Kubisch, who composed a piece that sounds like what a cat hears when it dreams.

Susie Ibarra.

Evelyn's hero Yoshimi P-We.

Harry Partch and his cloud bells, his giant marimbas like something out of *Honey, I Shrunk the Kids.*

Meredith Monk and the idea that music and dance have always been spiritual. That music can make spirituality a contemporary experience in a way that religion often fails to.

How a friendship can persist, in memory, as little more than a list of musicians and titles, because a list of music is a record of experience, of the sound-experience of a place and time.

Why did she like me? Not an irrelevant question, because the certainty that she liked me, and that other cool people I've known have liked me, has been my only reliable evidence, through the years, that I must be an interesting person. When my feelings about myself take a bad turn, this is the one proof that even my deepest insecurities can't controvert. Cool people aren't idiots, after all. You can't fool them into liking you. If they like you, then something about you must be at least a little bit likable.

She definitely liked me, we were definitely friends, in fact for a time she was my *best* friend, though I'm sure I wasn't hers. Not because she had closer friends, but because "best" was antithetical to all things Evelyn. That competitive possessiveness of "best." Is that why I've always wanted, from the earliest age, to have a "best" friend? Not because they would be "best," but because I would competitively possess them?

I sound like a terrible person!

I mean, jeez, I just wanted a best friend.

And anyway, she didn't have other "bests" either. Her favorite thing about music was its endless variety, and the idea of having a "favorite" song, for example, was antithetical to that. I keep using this word, antithetical. Evelyn didn't say antithetical. It sounds like a word I've lumped onto her. Probably I'm lumping all sorts of things onto her, coating her memory with a patina even more sparkling than the one she actually wore.

I mean, she *could* be kind of an asshole.

The time she attended an econ lecture. It was her idea. She listened, but I couldn't tell how much she was following. Afterward, she said, "Why are you interested in that?" Half judgy and half just wanting to understand.

"I'm good at it," I said honestly. "Sometimes the pleasure of doing something isn't so much in the thing itself, but just in the fact that you're good at it." I hadn't yet met Maggie, so I didn't have a better reason.

"I guess," she said, and we left it.

But later, maybe an hour later, long enough that it was odd the way she just picked the conversation back up again, she said, "It's like how rich people feel about making money." Somehow, I immediately knew what she was referring to, and what she meant. She meant that some rich people get rich because they're greedy, but some just like doing what they're

handling the music. She would set up on the landing halfway up the big wraparound staircase with her DJ stuff on one side and her drumkit on the other, then alternate sets between DJing and playing live with whoever showed up. It was half beat-thumping dance music and half free improvisation that only a really drunk person could dance to. It was brilliant. Everyone loved it. It's still hard to believe I was her friend.

But that time she showed up with a violin and asked me to perform with her. She knew I'd played violin in high school, but where she got a violin, and why she thought I would jump at this chance, I did not know then, and I still don't. She was very encouraging, everybody was—theater majors always so nice, friendly in a way that is borderline annoying—but I was thinking the whole time that I was not prepared for this, that I would not be any good at it, and that Evelyn could never understand why, for me, this situation was such a nightmare. She assumed I could play freely, as we did together in the percussion room. *All you need to do is listen and respond.* But "freely" in the percussion room is not "freely" in front of other people. Some of us, when we are in front of other people, retreat immediately to the things we've learned. To the comfort of structure, the prefab gestures of what you're "supposed" to do.

There I stood, deeply unhappy, on that makeshift stage next to Evelyn, who was amazing, feeling all of my inadequacies on display. I was hyper self-conscious, my brain working overtime, and what I was thinking was that actually Evelyn was wrong. She thought "freedom" was a matter of attitude, a rejection of training and talent. That a person with no training could theoretically be *freer*, because training just filled you with preconceptions about what music *ought to* be. But it was precisely Evelyn's training and talent that made her "freedom" sound so amazing. Ignorance doesn't make you good at anything. You don't free yourself by *un*learning. You have to learn *past* all you've learned. Whereas I was stuck in that awkward state of knowing just enough to feel embarrassed. I'd never been a good violinist, but I had enough music training to ruin any chance of being spontaneous in front of others.

Says the woman who has to "wing it" in front of a group of total strangers tomorrow.

It isn't self-consciousness but something like the opposite. You get up there and you go into automatic, like you're a passenger watching words come out of your mouth corresponding to thoughts ticker-taping through your brain. As if the thinking and speaking parts of your brain are occupying entirely different compartments, and there you'll be, there they'll be, you walk yourself through the rooms of your house, you mouth a speech until it's over. At which point it will not actually be over—it's only "over" until you realize it's still going—because here's the Q&A, which you think of yourself as good at. You think the Q&A is the easy part, but afterward you'll remember every word and feel weird about each one. Not because the words weren't good—if anything you'll admire the words while they're escaping your mouth. No, you'll feel bad that there were words coming out of you at all. That you let them escape your body, where they were at least safe. You exposed the world to your words. You exposed *your words* to *the world*. You feel exposed. Something has been given out that should have been kept in, because it was private. You are private. No one is allowed to be private anymore. Twitter feeds. Profile pics. TED talks. You enjoy speaking your ideas but you also hate it, and finally you hate it more than you enjoy it. Hearing yourself form words and project them toward people, who will probably not care much anyway. Who might at best watch curiously as your words sail past them and bounce off the back wall.

Keynes had his own Evelyn. János Plesch. What a name. Like a portmanteau of "plush" and "flesh." Which, yuck?

János Plesch was a Jewish Hungarian doctor, a blood specialist. He invented a device for taking blood pressure. He treated a lot of famous people: Trotsky, Strauss, the pope. He worked in Germany but escaped for England after the Nazis took power, and somehow met Keynes. One of those fascinating personalities that history has largely left behind. Known these days for a couple of chapters in his memoir where he wrote about Einstein, who was his lifelong patient and friend.

They came from different worlds, Plesch and Keynes, but they had in common an attitude toward experience, toward life. They both thought language and personality were crucial to their respective disciplines, as crucial as any math or science, that words shaped the world economy and the human body, both. They believed in improvisation, in trying things out, in not being afraid to change your mind, your methods. They were *careful*, of course—they weren't *cavalier*—just that they refused to accept without question what everyone else seemed to know. Plesch was against convalescence. He believed the body needs to be pushed. Above all, he believed in action, for his patients and himself. Like Keynes and monetary policy. The human body and the body politic. No wonder they got along.

It was Plesch who in the late '30s diagnosed and successfully treated the streptococci in Keynes's throat, prescribing an experimental predecessor to penicillin. Win one for experiment! Win one for risk! Unfortunately, he missed the streptococci in Keynes's heart, or his treatment did, and Keynes was dead a few years later.

This is the person I compare to Evelyn?

The end of our friendship did not happen all at once or even quite "happen" at all, though it seems that over the years I've come to think of it as having a definite end point. A point long prior to her death, which, it suddenly occurs to me, is probably why my memory ends our friendship earlier. To put safe distance between those two endings. To water down the finality.

It was senior year, those exciting few days before the semester gets going, when everyone's back but nothing's started. I was supposed to meet her at a party that night, but she took the bus and came over to my place early. I'd moved off campus, to the old house with the big back porch next to the gas station. You could sit on the porch and watch, over the wall, the round sign rotating on its pole. She simply showed up. She'd been in Brazil all summer, staying with family. She'd wanted to take an ethnomusicology class but it hadn't worked out, so instead she'd gone around on her own, meeting musicians, having adventures, every bit of which she was ready to recount for me. We talked in the kitchen for a while before she took out a bag of shriveled-up psychedelic mushrooms, which she wanted us to eat. It was the first time anyone ever offered me any drug other than pot, and I think I was a little bit flattered, just as I'd felt flattered freshmen year when someone first offered me pot. That I, Abby, could be mistaken for a person you simply offer pot to.

But I hadn't been expecting to eat mushrooms that night. I was not against having a new drug experience, but I had a pretty clear idea of what made a drug experience good or bad, and one of the few factors you could control was whether or not you planned it ahead of time. Spontaneity was not really my thing, in drug experiences. Or, frankly, in life. Spontaneity is not the same as improvisation—in fact they are almost opposites. Improvisation is a form of thought, a process of inventive reasoning, reasoning that plays outside the lines of Reason, but spontaneity is more like faith. Improvisation is a way of exploring the emotional and intellectual possibilities in a set of ideas and forms, but spontaneity rejects form and fetishizes risk. And drug experiences, while often really interesting, are also serious shit. In college, I was drawn to creativity and possibility. I was not boring. I am not boring. But I am also not, and wasn't then, and never will be, interested in risk for its own sake. I am drawn to risk as an expression of responsibility. Risk as the spirit of courage you bring to things you truly care about. Evelyn, I cared about. Psychedelic mushrooms, on the other hand, were dried fungus that smelled gross and reportedly made your stomach hurt.

But this was college, so, yes, of course, I ate the mushrooms. I made a salad and smothered them in green goddess dressing. We sat out on the porch. They tasted like dirt. All the green goddess in the world could not have made them taste any better. Oh well. We were going to a party.

It had been a weird week. Earlier that week, Mr. Jin, my landlord, who was well into his seventies, had died suddenly of a heart attack. I hadn't seen Mrs. Jin yet. I don't know how I'd learned the news. As part of my rental agreement, I'd been driving Mr. Jin to the grocery store once a week, an odd arrangement that I told myself was a healthy counterpoint to college, a chance to emerge from my social cocoon and rediscover the outside world. He was naturally chatty, Mr. Jin. If he hadn't been so old, I would have thought he was flirting with me. Mrs. Jin must have thought so, since whenever I delivered him home, she would stare at us suspiciously. The whole thing might have been funny, my tiny soap opera with an elderly Korean couple, were it not for how abruptly Mr. Jin would shut her down with a look. She was a formidable woman,

Mrs. Jin. On her own, discussing the rent, or whatever was bugging her that week, she could be downright intimidating, so the way she cowered at these sharp looks from her husband was unnerving. Otherwise, they seemed to get along. And really, it was none of my business. They'd lived their whole lives together. I was just the chauffeur.

Now Mr. Jin was dead. Sitting on the porch with Evelyn, the porch I rented from Mr. and Mrs. Jin, one of whom was now dead, waiting for the dirt-tasting mushrooms to kick in, I wondered what would happen with him gone. Would Mrs. Jin be nicer to me? Would I start taking her to the grocery store?

Then at some point, consciousness had noticeably shifted and Evelyn and I were walking, up through the large hilly cemetery that stood between that old house and campus. I understood the situation of my mind well enough to know that there was no way I was getting on a bus. We were side by side, talking about everything and nothing, about whatever interesting sensations or perceptions we were experiencing. Psychedelic mushroom talk. Early evening cemetery talk. Cool cemetery air is always delicious, air of trees and open spaces, of paved paths with benches, groves of pillars and stones. A cemetery is a whole small world inside our larger one, with its own exotic inhabitants. Living people are the ghosts here. We pass through their domain imperceptibly, outside of the reality they occupy. Their society meets across history, across time. Time is a form of space to them, a perpetual simultaneity. They have so much to say to one another, but no way to talk!

And so on.

The plan was: cemetery to neighborhood, neighborhood to campus, through campus to the party in the neighborhood beyond. Yet by the time we reached campus many eons had passed, and that plan already seemed very distant. A plan made in a different lifetime, by an earlier generation, handed down but no longer fully comprehended. Like the generations of space-travelers it would take to reach the closest star. With each generation, the memory of Earth would grow more remote, more mythic. By the time their great-grandchildren finally arrived, they would look out at this new, basically identical patch of space, and say, "Does anybody remember why we were going to Alpha Centauri?"

And so on.

At some point we were in the percussion room, playing all the different instruments. Eventually we moved on, probably several times, though always with a feeling of *somehow*. Somehow, we were in one place, then somehow we'd arrived at another. Somehow I had met Evelyn, and our journeys through life had overlapped. Somehow—incredibly—that had happened. But we would both get older, and would become different people than we were now. The people we'd become would be in some ways exactly what we imagined, and in other ways not at all. Someday I would think back on this night with Evelyn—or the person I would become would think back—and it would have meant something. That much I knew. That this future self would be lying in a creaky hotel bed in an unfamiliar city, next to a husband and a daughter, I did not yet know. Or that Evelyn would be dead, that she would die several years later and hundreds of miles away, and I would not even know how she died. That I would not even have anyone to contact to ask how she died.

The mind is a big murky lake, and sometimes you have to just jump in and hope there aren't large jagged rocks under the surface. It's easy to be skeptical of the thoughts you've had while tripping, to write them off as mere mushroom talk, but your mushroom mind isn't always wrong. Your mushroom mind sees some things more clearly than your sober mind ever will. Sees things as they are, and welcomes them. Your insomnia mind is more like your mushroom mind, in that respect. But your mushroom mind is mostly benevolent, while your insomnia mind is out to destroy you. It's your job to tell it, *No*. Not tonight.

Not tonight, insomnia mind.

Very late, we ended up at the party, which we must have known we would eventually reach. Evelyn walked in first, and by the time I got my bearings, she was already out of the room, she'd wandered off, in what direction I didn't know. And the whole place was instantly too much, too loud, so I slipped into a corner and stayed there, not freaking out but not happy either, while people moved around me. Big human blur. Wondering where Evelyn had disappeared to. Wanting to leave, but not without her. Having whatever increasingly exasperated thoughts I was having, while over and over she

not need me, I thought. I was happy where I was. It wasn't personal. Or everything was. Experience itself was personal, a thing you could never share with anyone else, not really. You could try. You could overlap with another person, your experiences of the world could briefly coincide in time and space and in that sense feel shared. You could have friends. But only you could ever know what the world felt like to you. And you could never know what the world felt like to another person. In that sense, you were always alone. Which was fine, though. Everything was fine. Everything was exactly the way it was, and I was okay. I felt connected to the lives in the houses I passed, all those dark windows, people gone to bed hours ago. I felt generous toward them, even while acknowledging what an empty gesture my generosity was. What an empty gesture my goodwill toward anyone was, since it was all just a feeling. Mushroom emotions. Much the way, in my sober life, I was completely aware of my existence as a middle-class suburban American whose tastes had been shaped by legions of advertising agents, graphic designers, and media influencers, but I didn't do much about it. I changed what I could but accepted the rest, because some social constructs you need to accept. Consciously or unconsciously, every day you decide which constructs to accept and which to question, about yourself and about the world. You can't question everything. You should work on yourself, be aware of yourself, try to better yourself, but you can't always treat yourself as the problem. Life is hard enough. You were born into a homogenous wasteland, a society that champions sameness but treats people differently, a culture orchestrated to sell you things. You found a way out, a way of understanding yourself and growing, of breaking through intellectual boundaries, but you carried forth from your upbringing a deep-seated resistance to other sorts of messiness—emotional, interpersonal—and fear of confrontation in any form. You enjoy a theoretical generosity toward humanity, but in many ways you are kind of an asshole. You left Evelyn at that party. How long did you even wait? It might have been hours, but it was probably more like ten minutes. Then you left without looking. That was what happened back there. That was the person you were.

And so on.

I turned a corner and stopped. I'd thought I was wandering aimlessly, heading vaguely in the direction of my house, but now I saw that I had *arrived* somewhere much too purposeful to have landed there at random. A small box of a house, two squat stories, with ornamental shutters and a metal roof, which I immediately recognized as my landlord's house. The house of Mr. and Mrs. Jin. One of whom, I suddenly remembered, was dead. Mr. Jin was dead. Poor Mrs. Jin.

All the front blinds were closed, but blue light flickered behind the downstairs picture window. Was there anything more lonely-seeming, to my undergraduate self, than the light of a television flickering behind window blinds late at night? I knew from having been inside what the room behind those blinds looked like. The white rug and bronze lamps. I knew that the sofa was right under the window, with the television opposite in the corner. I could picture that room perfectly well. Mrs. Jin was in there, all alone on the sofa, unable to sleep. Staring at whatever stupid thing was playing on the television. Her husband, her partner of a lifetime, had died. She was filled with feelings I could not even begin to imagine or understand. There is nothing I can do for her, I thought, there is nothing we can do for each other, in the end we are all alone. But my body still felt heavy, swollen with the knowledge of Mrs. Jin's loneliness. I wasn't melancholic. I would not allow myself to feel generous. I was witnessing her solitude, just bearing witness. I felt also, for the first time that evening, the pinch of my own deep loneliness, never far from me in those days, always just out past the edge of my so-called self-awareness.

At which point, or very shortly after, I did an incredibly stupid thing.

Which may also have been the best thing I ever did.

Other than Ali, of course.

Because I *knew* how stupid it was, even going in. How bound it was to end badly. But I risked it, I took what seemed at the time an incredible risk, knowing perfectly well that I was in no frame of mind to make good or reasonable decisions. *Knowing* that my mindset was fooling me and that following it made me a fool. I *expected* it to be a catastrophe.

But it wasn't. It was wonderful.

"Poor Mrs. Jin," I thought, "all alone in there. Unable to sleep, unable to read or concentrate, stuck with only a stupid TV for company, a TV playing who knows what garbage at this hour. Staring at that stupid TV's stupid garbage and seeing there, in the screen, in whatever sitcom rerun or news recap, a depiction of her own loneliness, her all-aloneness, now that her husband has died. Poor, poor Mrs. Jin.

"And here I am, a human being who knows her, a friend, in a way, or at least someone who wishes her well. Here I am also awake, also alone, standing just a few feet away, separated by nothing but a small stretch of lawn and a door. But separated also by social convention, by the late hour, the odd circumstances, an impossible distance to cross. I look at the blue flickers and I know she's in there suffering, but there's nothing I can do for her. How easy it would be to reach out to her! Yet how impossible!

"*This* is what's wrong with the world. Purely and simply wrong. That two people who are alone and who know each other can't manage to reach out to one another, to offer company, because of the hour and the roles we play. Landlady. Tenant. Stupid roles for a stupid world. Stupid rules! We force ourselves to follow them, but we're the ones who suffer.

"In a better world, a more just world, I would simply go up to that door and knock. She would answer and be surprised to see me. She would act baffled, but I would see, too, that she was pleased. That as surprising as my presence was, it also made perfect sense to her. I would say that I'd simply been out walking, unable to sleep. That I was out for a walk and saw the blue light in her window, and figured she was still awake. That I thought, if she's awake, then in that case perhaps we might keep each other company . . ."

Who knows how long I stood in that street, debating whether or not it was in my power, for one brief moment, to push back against the loneliness of existence. Reminding myself that I was tripping on mushrooms and wondering how different my thoughts would be if I weren't. How much less foolish I would be. How much less brave! I do not remember crossing Mrs. Jin's lawn, but I have a distinct memory of knocking, then waiting.

It took a minute for her to answer.

I'm getting chills just thinking about this.

"Abigail," she said. "What time is it?" Rubbing her eyes. She'd been sleeping! She'd fallen asleep in front of the TV, probably hours earlier, and my knocking woke her up.

"Mrs. Jin!" I said. "I was just out walking and saw your lights on!"

"Are you drunk?"

"I didn't mean to disturb you! I just thought you might be up!"

"Your face is all red. You've been drinking."

"No, no. I was in the park today! I got a terrible sunburn!"

"That's a sunburn?"

"A really bad sunburn!"

"That's not a sunburn. Your face is red like a cherry."

"I was just walking by and saw your TV was on!"

"You've been drinking. It's okay. Come in. I'll make you tea."

So in I went, and she closed the door, and after that I was so completely in the present that I can't really remember any of it. Like at my wedding—I remember all our family and friends showing up, and the music starting, then: *blur*. By the time my brain slowed down enough to register itself, the reception was almost over and Ed and I were getting in a car. It's not that you fail to pay attention in such moments, but that you pay so much attention there's no room for anything else. The present overwhelms you. Probably I was worried the whole time that Mrs. Jin would figure me out. I must have felt relief that she assumed I was drunk, since the reality would have been so much worse to her. I know I was there until it started being light out. And we drank tea together, and talked, and it felt like a moment between friends. I also know that by the time I left, not only was I sober, but I was quite certain that, against all odds, the visit had been a success. True, I had woken her up, had imposed my inebriated romanticism upon her very real mourning, had embarrassed myself and inconvenienced her in wildly inappropriate ways, but Mrs. Jin was glad I'd come. The stupid idealistic risk I'd taken had miraculously paid off. Because she was lonely. Because even if I was stupid, I wasn't *wrong*.

In fact, I was courageous, I thought, as I headed back to my house, though now that I'm approaching the end of this memory, I am starting to doubt it's the inspiring story I remembered it being. At the time, I was certain my intrusion that night had been a special moment for both of us, that I'd done something real, something brave, and that it was me, Abby, who had done it. I got home and cooked eggs and ate them on the porch, looking back across the hours since Evelyn had shown up with her baggie of shriveled mushrooms. I told myself I'd had an important experience, and that life would be different now. Something was bound to change.

All of which may have been true for *me*, but why was I so sure, why have I felt sure until just this moment, that the experience was any good for Mrs. Jin? More likely my intrusion that night was a terrible imposition. Why didn't I see this before? Or Evelyn—why wasn't I a better friend to her that night? Weirdest of all, most inexplicable of all, why am I suddenly getting worked up about this? All of this happened many years ago. All of this is *gone*. Yet here again comes the cringing, the random kicks of memory-adrenaline that make your toes crimp, that make your fingers dig into your palms, as if something terrible is happening *right now*. Terrible things are always happening, but they aren't always tied to your feelings. You have *feelings* about nonsense, about stuff that doesn't matter, while ignoring countless terrible *things*.

Stop! You have to stop.

Events that happened years ago, that are utterly lost to the past and have no consequences for the present, should *not* hit you in the middle of the night with an onrush of shame and self-loathing.

Mistakes made when you were young that barely even mattered at the time should *not* revisit you years later and make your whole body cringe.

There needs to be a statute of limitations.

After that my life did change—that much I was right about—though I'm not sure those changes had much to do with Evelyn or Mrs. Jin. It was around then that I met Ed and we started spending time together. And I took that class with Maggie. With one thing and another, I hung out with Evelyn less and less. That our friendship fizzled away was more my doing than hers, since the effort of maintaining it had always fallen to me. Evelyn was self-contained. She had friends everywhere. She stayed the same, or seemed to, while I moved on. Probably it happened so gradually that neither of us noticed.

The truth is that for all my insecurities, I've never had any problem leaving things behind. Even people I've cared about. Before Ed and Ali, I could walk away from anyone or anything. For most of my life, I assumed this was hardwired, a kind of inbred coldness, but I am no longer that person. Ed and Ali are proof of that. They're the reason for it. Ed and Ali and getting older and caring about different things. The person I was before wouldn't lie here sleepless and unhappy. She would get up right now, waking whoever she happened to wake. She'd throw on some clothes and walk around the hotel. She'd sit in the lobby with a notebook staring out a dark window at the unfamiliar streets of this city, wondering what's out there. If there was coffee available in the lobby, she would give up on the possibility of sleep and go ahead and have a cup of coffee. She would sit hunched over her coffee, with her notebook, in love with her loneliness. As if the coffee and the notebook and the unfamiliar city were proof of something special about herself. *That* Abby found herself much more interesting than I find myself now. But I prefer this Abby to that one.

After college, Evelyn moved to San Francisco. The last I heard, she'd become a very successful DJ and performer, which made perfect sense. I could picture her presiding over a club or dance hall, leading this giant room full of excited people in an improvisational ballet of sound and light and movement, allowing everyone to feel, for a moment, part of something special. It was good to be able to think that her energy and beauty were out there in the world, doing those things, even if I was no longer a part of it. Then she died, and that was a shock. Ed saw it in an alumni e-newsletter. He called me in and showed me. I didn't even have anybody to call.

I hadn't thought about her much in years, hadn't missed her, so the overwhelming effect of her death did not make sense. My reaction didn't seem, to me, like a reasonable reaction to the death of someone by then so distant. I wasn't just upset. It was like the ground was gone. I'd never felt that way before. Not that death was new to me—I'd known people my age who had died, people from high school, another friend from college, though nobody close. Of course, it's possible my feelings for Evelyn were simply more complicated than I'd thought. Whatever the reason, for a week after her death, I had the same terrifying dream every night. I would wake up gasping, a kind of panic I'd never known. Ed got really worried about it. So did I. We talked about my going to see someone, but then the nightmare went away. I've never dreamt it again, though sometimes I still think about it. When I think about it, I can feel it again. I can remember, in my body, the horrible feeling the dream caused me to feel.

A dark basement, cinder block walls, and there's a door here, blue. A blue doorframe wedged roughly into the wall, sloppily caulked into the cinder blocks. Push open the door, and the room beyond is just a space, a mouth. I can't see inside at all. I walk through the doorway and the effect is like holding down the brightness button on a dark computer screen, there's nothing and then, suddenly, light rushes in. I see that this side of the basement is painted entirely black, even the floor and ceiling, with black-painted pipes running into and out of the walls, and clanking noises. Evelyn is standing in front of me, her hand extended toward me. In the dream, I know that she's dead. The light is natural light, not lightbulb light, from a window along the ceiling over Evelyn's left shoulder. The black walls and pipes look a little glossy, the black paint reflects the light, but the black of the ceiling and floor swallows the light, as if there is nothing there but empty space. Then I realize that Evelyn's hand is not extended to me, but is pointing past me, to the floor. I turn, and there lying dead on the floor behind me is a large white dog. It is not a particular breed, just large and white. It has a red bandana tied around its neck as decoration, and it's lying on its side, not breathing. It looks stiff. I don't approach it. A sentence comes into my head, the same words every time: *A white dog lies dead on the floor of a black basement.* I turn back to Evelyn and she's still facing me. She mouths some words, though no sound comes out, but I understand the words anyway. Sometimes the words are "That's me," and sometimes "I'm dead." Those are the only two things she ever says, either one or the other. But the moment she speaks these words, panic pours into my body, like water from a pitcher, quickly filling up my feet, my legs, then my torso and arms, my neck, all the way to the top of my head. I find myself suffocating inside my own body. But I am also, while this is happening, calm. Because in the dream, I know that this is *me*, now, forever. This feeling. *A white dog lies dead on the floor of a black basement.* I will live inside this feeling forever.

8

f I'm not more careful, I will make myself very unhappy.

If I keep letting everything into my head, I'll be awake like this all night.

Why did I want to *remember* things?

History is the nightmare from which I am trying to fall asleep.

9

Finally, we arrive at the door to my office. Those were some long and treacherous stairs. Remind me to take the elevator next time.

"Obviously, you do not have an elevator."

Keynes! I won't have an office much longer, either.

"So melodramatic."

That's what happens when you leave me alone for too long.

"Whose fault is that?"

I just mean that you're a calming influence.

"I should hope so. It's the only reason I'm here."

You're here to keep me company.

"Same difference."

And to keep me on track.

"How has that been going?"

And because I always work better with feedback, but Ed is asleep.

"You rely on him for feedback."

It helps.

"Except that I, being you, am not 'feedback.' I'm a sounding board."

So?

"So, if I am standing in for Ed, that suggests that what you rely on him for is not really to give feedback, but only to be a sounding board."

I think he understands that.

"What he perhaps does not understand is that you do not really even need him as a sounding board. Evidently, you can do 'sounding board' all by yourself."

He's a very good sounding board. Things sound better bounced off of him than off of other surfaces.

"Acoustical Ed."

Also loving.

"Acoustical, also loving, Ed."

Men have done worse.

"Much worse."

Now stop talking.

I am in my office.

A converted sunroom, small but spacious. All-white walls. Wood floor. Great big windows along two sides. Simple white curtains. Plain office chair and work desk with computer and piles of books on one side of the room. Cozy reading chair on the other. A half bookshelf, chest-high, next to a door that leads to a closet. A few leafy plants. And a really tall floor lamp that rises up over the cozy chair from behind. That's all. That's *it*. Nothing else in this room. Airy as an operating theater, clean as a very clean kitchen. Clean *feeling* anyway—I can't remember the last time I actually cleaned it. A writing room. A reading and thinking room. A "room of one's own"—which was my first Virginia Woolf book, incidentally, and remains a favorite example of how a conceptual argument—in this case about female autonomy, living your own life—can also be a practical argument, in a way Keynes probably appreciated. A woman's autonomy is not just about rights or laws, she's saying. A woman literally needs her own room.

She was your friend, Keynes. You were housemates and friends. Then she drowned herself. How did you feel when you heard about it?

"We were close," says Keynes, who is standing by the closet door with one hand on the bookshelf. "There were always falling-outs among the Bloomsbury people, but Leonard and Virginia and I stayed friends. Even after Lydia and I moved to the country, we spent Christmases together."

It must have been very sad. And confusing. The death of a very gifted person is strange for their friends, even if they haven't seen each other for a while. Trying to balance, emotionally, the cost to the world and the cost to yourself. The feeling that you lost something all your own, alongside the feeling that the culture, which is also yours, lost something as well. Two losses that overlap but are fundamentally different. That in some ways might even contend with one another, yet you have to make sense of them together.

"Enough about death," says Keynes. He's impatient with me. I'm impatient with myself. "Death is not your topic."

Because I am in my office.

"Yes."

Where I've come to deliver the portion of my speech about utopia.

"Exactly."

What's interesting is that if I were home, this is where I *would* be now. My office. Having crept out of bed as quietly as possible, making the least possible noise with our old creaky doors. Having snuck away from the mental tailspin of my insomnia without waking a soul. Ensconced in this cozy chair in my office, in the light of that overhanging lamp. A pocket of light to sit snugly inside of, beside the dark windows. Listening to the distant sound of cars on the highway, like the *shush* of faraway trains I used to hear in bed growing up. Trains that must have been very far away indeed, since there were no tracks near our neighborhood. People going places and doing things. How many people live that way, train conductors and convenience store clerks, night watchmen and third-shift factory workers, all up and walking around doing things, their whole lives lived at night. While here in my cozy office at this solitary hour, I would be reading or writing in a notebook, emptying my mind of all the noise accumulated while lying sleepless over there in the bedroom. Reading and writing being the only good methods I have ever found for emptying my insomnia mind, and calming it. Watching TV doesn't work. Nothing with a screen. Even being up with Ed rarely manages to cut through the noise of whatever happens to be bothering me. But for some reason reading works, reading in particular. The mental release, the distraction, or maybe just the voice, the company. Back in grad school, when I woke up in the middle of the night, I would turn on the light and read Keynes's essays about economic problems from decades ago, essays whose arguments had often been proven wrong by time, but I read them despite wrongness, despite datedness, for the voice of the person writing. His voice, his astuteness and humor, his crabbiness, the *life* in his voice, his way of seeing and thinking about the world that was not just in the ideas or claims or arguments but in the way the voice *thought*, the way the thoughts turned, *Every style is a means of insisting on something*, said Susan Sontag. Reading essays on economics for the life in the language. The life in the language being the only reason some of those essays even mattered anymore. And if that was true, if the life in the language was the only reason some of that writing still mattered, then it followed that the life in the language was a large part of why they'd mattered in the first place, back when Keynes wrote them. This epiphany: that so much of what I cared about in Keynes was the person in the words. The company. A 3:00 a.m. thought that turned into a thesis. Economics is made out of language and serves all the purposes that language serves, the persuasive and the performative, the communicative, the utopian, the beautiful. The companionable. Speaking as a way of sharing. Sharing as a way of seeing.

In the cozy chair by the windows surrounded by simple things in a pocket of soft light, I would be feeling much better right now. Because as much as I hate lying sleepless in bed, that much do I love spending those same sleepless moments in my office. How easily worries and doubts turn into delicious solitude, its own blankety warmth. When you know you are loved but not trapped. How effortlessly your writing mind exhales its pettiness, how quickly your reading mind breathes in new replenishing ideas, how successfully you staunch all this, this stewing.

In my office late at night, words come easily. Ideas spill out and for the most part make sense. A single thought doesn't stick in the same spot but moves on to make room for a new one. In my office late at night I am freer, more filled with possibility, than in any other place at any other time, but awake here, in this mediocre hotel room that I can't even see, that I just know is out there around me, a wallpapered box with thick furniture—awake *here* fills my mind with nonsense, leaving space for nothing new. Thoughts fester. Thought festers. Thinks fall apart.

If Ed and Ali hadn't come with me, this moment would be different. If they'd stayed home like they probably wanted to. I would turn on the light and open a book, I would walk around the hotel, it would feel good to be up and reading or walking. Not good like in my office at home, but better than this. Of course, I would feel lonely away from them, which is obviously why I forced them to come. I can't imagine any other reason. I didn't want to be alone so I put them in the room with me, and it is better, it's definitely better in *that* sense. But it also means I'm stuck here having to deal with myself. Which is perhaps a special case of the general theory of having a family at all. It makes you less crazy than you'd otherwise be, but it doesn't allow you to get as crazy as you sometimes need to.

Plus, there's the love.

None of which is my topic. Insomnia is not my topic. Cozy lamplight is not my topic. Family is not. Crazy is not. Love is not.

I have come here to talk about utopia.

The most immediately interesting thing about the word "utopia" is that almost nobody uses it correctly. The word comes into the language from Sir Thomas More, who in the early sixteenth century wrote a book about a remote island whose civilization had very different customs, habits, and social and governing systems from the ones practiced in Europe at the time. He called this place Utopia, a combination of the prefix *ou* and the Greek word *topos*, which translates as "no place"—as in, a place that doesn't exist—but which also calls to mind its homophone *eutopia*, which means "good place," which is what most people these days think "utopia" means.

The chief characteristic of Thomas More's Utopia is the abolition of all private property, and all money. There's still a social hierarchy, but it's based on virtue and education rather than wealth. There are lots of other differences—the whole book is essentially a list of all the things the Utopians do differently than sixteenth-century Europeans—but the removal of private property is the big one, because it addresses what More sees as the central issue of humanity, the "parent of all plagues," his *permanent problem*, which is pride. "Pride" in the sense of needing to be better than other people, which I guess is more like vanity. Four hundred years later, as I mentioned way back there in my living room, Keynes divided "goods" into things we need and things we simply want, saying that the future will fulfill all of our *needs*, but we'll still be stuck with our wants. Being an optimist about human nature, he seems unconcerned that our "wants" will define us. I tried to suggest that Keynes's arguably naïve outlook could be blamed on the fact that he was writing prior to the incredible rise of mass mediation and the manipulation of our "wants" by the advertising industry, but this defense, if it's a defense, fails to account for the fact that four hundred years earlier, Thomas More was already taking a more pessimistic view. He thought most Europeans of his day cared more about one-upping their neighbors than about having the basic things they needed, and he blamed this on private property and money. As long he wouldn't even comprehend it, except for the part where government officials in Utopia are held entirely above the law—that part he'd love—their reasoning being that in order to become a government official you have to be a really good person, so the chances of having a corrupt one are almost nil. I mean, why didn't we think of that?

I seem to have mixed feelings about the Utopians. Also, I'm blathering. Among the good things in Utopia are religious freedom, multigenerational family living, and a six-hour workday, which is possible because everybody works, and it turns out that when you have no concept of private property, or any rich people to horde it, there is plenty of everything to go around. With the aforementioned exceptions, people are treated equally, and if there are a lot of rules limiting what Utopians are allowed to do, Sir Thomas More tries to make up for this by suggesting that in the absence of private property, and thus of greed, most of our vile pastimes wouldn't interest us anyway. Utopians are all for pleasure, but their primary pleasures are pooping, conjugal sex, and scratching an itch, in that order. They also do a lot of gardening, and attend educational lectures to better themselves. Educational lectures like this one! If you would all now give yourselves a thorough scratching and head off to enjoy a satisfying bowel movement, you'll be well on your way to a Utopian day.

The point of all this being only that Utopia was never a perfect place, or even necessarily a good one, though compared to sixteenth-century Europe it must have sounded pretty good.

Its real value—the real value of any utopia—is that it doesn't exist. It's not a model of how everything *should be*; it's an alternative to whatever reality you currently inhabit. The purpose of a utopia is to open your eyes to possibility, to allow yourself to see more clearly, by way of contrast, the society in which you live, the customs you've grown so accustomed to that they've come to seem inevitable. It's not a proposition, even less a plan, but a viable reminder that everything you take to be "the world" could be, if we wanted it to be, very different.

At this point I have a few paths I could take. I could go the hard-core philosophy route, in which case I would need to decide which philosopher to use. Ricoeur? *Ideology and Utopia.* I could cite from memory some easy-to-parse passage, like "Part of the literary strategy of utopia is to aim at persuading the reader by the rhetorical means of fiction," which would work well when I circle back to my original claim that Keynes's essay is not a proposal or prediction but a form of utopian storytelling, its purpose to counter the then-prevailing story that the Great Slump was coming, like some B-movie monster, to swallow European civilization in one Great Slumpy *slurp.* Though piling one term atop another might just gunk things up. It might sound like I'm saying a bunch of words.

I could crib some lines from Muñoz?

Or pretty much any Frankfurt-type philosopher.

Stuart Hall's "narrative construction of reality"?

Or I could steer clear of theory altogether and stick to examples. I could talk about feminist utopias, and why the imaginative subversive potential of the utopian mode is suited to the goals of feminism, a subject more accessible than "ideology"—I hope!—and with the added bonus of making clear that all of this is not just theoretical, it plays out everywhere in everyday life. I could use Bartkowski's ideas about spaces where *that which is not* becomes *what could be,* and this would make sense to anybody, because even an idiot can see how feminism's stories run counter to the stories we live by, here in the still-patriarchal present. I would have to be clear, though, that I was using feminist literary utopias only as an example, then back up to a more general understanding of utopias before drawing the comparison to Keynes. Which again feels like adding a whole layer to an argument that has too many layers already.

Ugh.

Or I could go full-out populist, as I've basically been doing this whole time, though that's because my topics haven't been as complicated. There hasn't been much nuance to lose. I could adopt the TED-talk style of that Rutger Bregman book, which was a perfectly fine book, yes, I have no problem admitting this, but which made me exceedingly angry, because it came out around the same time as my book, and makes many of the same arguments mine makes, but in these journalistic glosses and mainstream bon mots. And of course it sold *so* much better than mine. Wide-eyed Dutch guy who, on top of everything else, is younger than me. Watching that book get praised and fawned over. Universal basic income: how intriguing! Utopia in our lifetimes: sounds good! You know the one about Nixon's fiscal policy that never happened? What about *Speenhamland*? That's a funny word. Here's a quick jaunt through Thomas Piketty, an inspirational anecdote about the power of ideas!

Abigail, enough. Jealousy does not become you.

If I were a better person, I would be nothing but happy that these ideas made their way onto the bestseller list, no matter who wrote them down or how comestible he made them. They're not *my* ideas, after all, even if I thought them on my own. Ideas don't *belong* to anyone. And it's not like we both wrote the same book. Really, it was his inclusion of Keynes's essay that set me off. He didn't *see* "Economic Possibilities," didn't appreciate the historical and philosophical nuance of it. It didn't mean anything to him *personally*. He just threw it in there for good measure. Probably it was the fact that he'd just thrown it in there that made me feel—what? That he'd stolen it from me. Not stolen in a legal way, but the way somebody in high school steals your boyfriend. Hands off, Bregman!

Not that Bregman's even my competition. Do I have competition? Since when is the life of the mind a competition? Worse was seeing McCloskey give that YouTube talk in Italy. Boy, did that push my buttons. I'm getting worked up just thinking about it. Hundreds of millions of people will lose their jobs to robots in the next ten years, but on YouTube, ladies and gentlemen, you can find the very smart Christian libertarian economic historian Deirdre McCloskey telling an audience in Italy not to worry about it. I happened to stumble upon this on my laptop lying in bed in my pajamas almost immediately after learning I'd just been unburdened of my own quote-unquote career. Historically the economy always adjusts to technology, goes the argument. People find new and different jobs. Humans invented agriculture, then moved from agriculture to industry, from industry to service, the jobs keep moving and the standard of living keeps going up. It reminded me of a conversation on NPR about how prehistoric dogs stopped hunting and reinvented themselves as pets. It was an episode on early retirement! Or that Perry Farrell song about humans making great pets, a song I could never get out of my head once it got stuck in there—well don't think about it *now*—though I'm pretty sure that song is about Martian takeover rather than large-scale job displacement. McCloskey not really addressing, at least in the part of the video I watched, which let's be honest was only the first ten minutes, that standard of living in the way we currently construe it is a fairly awful measure of the actual *quality of life*, and that endless growth has turned out to have some sizable problems of its own. A point that Keynes *also* fails to make in "Economic Possibilities for Our Grandchildren"—remember to make a bigger deal of that under "shortcomings"—and which seems to me—the failure to make that point seems to me—tone-deaf to the actual experience of living in our present state of environmental depletion and our caste culture of economic bullying. In fact, during the ten minutes I sat stewing in bed in my pajamas watching that video, it occurred

alternative, a "no place" with habits and presumptions different from ours, we can better understand the constructed nature of our own stories, and decide for ourselves whether we are telling them as well as we could be. Like the story of how a nation is an actual thing, rather than an idea people collectively agree to—are we telling that one as well as we could? Or the story that money is valuable, when really it's the *story* of money that we place value in. All the stories about how you're supposed to act, what men are supposed to be like, or women are supposed to be like, what people in general are supposed to be like. These examples are already getting vague. The stories you accept, the ones you question, the ones you don't believe but still need in order to get through the day. Like the story that we're all going to get our acts together on climate change before it's too late. That is one I personally need in order to get through the day. The story that guns make us safer. That is one I don't believe at all but am forced to hope I am wrong about. The story that—what? These should be rolling off my tongue. That actors' lives are interesting. That scientists are handling it. That education improves our personalities. Now we're getting somewhere. The story that success only counts if it's measurable. That the more papers you publish, the smarter you must be. That if the economy is growing, everyone benefits. The story that giving poor people a guaranteed income will make them lazy. That rich people earned what they have. The story that. The story. Well, that's probably enough examples anyway. That the future is an uphill climb, there's hope on the horizon, a light at the end of the tunnel. That our children will be better than us. That they will make up for our mistakes. The story that Ali's future will be full of golden opportunities, blue skies, and endless well-being. Or rather, since that story is a stretch for even a Keynes-sized optimist, the story that somehow Ali will manage to create a meaningful existence despite living in a world that is increasingly hot, increasingly crowded, and increasingly privatized. Increasingly sexist, racist, gun-toting, pharmaceutical, food-processed, and focus-grouped. Biohazardous, natural-disastered. Garbage-dumped chemical-fertilized deforested diseased. Increasingly plugged in. Increasingly stressed out. Screen-timed. Hacked. Increasingly unlivable. Unlivably unlikable. Liveunable. Unilaterally collateral. Livlivily unlovable. Tired. I am *so* tired. I am utterly exhausted. In general in life, but in particular all of a sudden right now. Wasted. Spent. Heavy-headed. Heavy-lidded. I was chugging right along when all of a sudden this whole long night crashed down on top of me. Maybe I'll fall asleep in the middle of listing catastrophes. Wouldn't that be embarrassing. Talk about disaffected. I blame capitalism. Or television. Who am I kidding I

10

—what?

Just nodded off. Did I?

If you don't think, if you relax into it, maybe you can get back there.

Hurry up and relax!

And now I am awake again.

The worst thing to do is worry. I have enough worries without worrying about falling asleep. And don't I always eventually anyway? Even on the worst nights, I finally drift off, then have these terribly intense dreams in the tiny interval before the alarm clock rips me awake. Instead of worrying about sleeping, I should be consoling myself with the fact that I've never been *able* to stay awake all night. At some point, the impossible becomes inevitable.

That time I went to a sleepover across the street and three houses down. Cindy something. Mom said she's a comptroller now. Which sounds like a giant robot but is in fact a municipal accountant. I went to her sleepover and all the other kids, her friends from private school, said that whoever fell asleep first would get their hand put in a glass of warm water, to make them pee. So, of course, I tried to stay awake. I tried my very hardest, I mentally pinched myself all over to stay awake, but I still woke up in the middle of the night with a wet sleeping bag. How old was I? Too old for that! It taught me a very important lesson: *avoid kids from private school*. But it did not teach me to stay awake. I've still never gone an entire night without sleep.

That's not true.

Twice in my life I stayed up the whole night. The second time was that night I took mushrooms with Evelyn and woke up Mrs. Jin, and the first was in high school, when I attempted to go to prom with Jason Gustafson. That would have been junior not senior year, because it was at the start of our friendship. It was why our friendship got off to such a rocky start.

Jason Gustafson who I haven't thought about in ages, though I suppose he was also an important person for me.

I suppose he shaped the person I became as much as anybody did.

As much as Maggie or Evelyn, not because he was anything like a role model—as if!—but only because he came into my life earlier.

The effects he caused became the causes of later effects.

Violin. Fountains. Minivan. Texas.

Agenbite of outwit.

Nitwit.

Weird feelings.

Why does everything from high school seem dumb and embarrassing?

Whenever my mind turns to my teenage years, which is almost never, but on the off times it occasionally does, and I try to decide whether or not thinking about those years is worth the energy, I experience something like the opposite of nostalgia. I am hit with a very strong sense that high school was dumb and embarrassing.

Also dull.

"If it's as dull as you suggest," offers Keynes—standing where? Wait, where are we? Are we still in my office? "If thinking about high school is as dull as you suggest," Keynes says, "perhaps it will put you back to sleep?"

So this is what my life has been reduced to.

What the vast expanses of my past boil down to.

A soporific.

Once upon a time, I had a ten-second crush on an odd, self-absorbed, basically nice, occasionally interesting guy. Interesting for high school. He played the violin in our school's twelve-person string ensemble, and since I also played violin in that minuscule ensemble, we knew each other.

In fact, I'd been curious about him for a few years, though I never really let on. Because I was quiet? Because he was a hard person to make sense of. He read books and seemed to know a lot, but he could be fairly dorky. "Agenbite of outwit!" was what he said to me when I asked why he didn't just get his own electric tuner, since he kept borrowing mine. That was before we really knew each other, and for whatever reason "Agenbite of outwit!" made an impression. Maybe because he didn't explain it. He just acted like I was supposed to know what it meant. The lure of the abstruse. I was curious enough to look it up later, but too lazy to persist when my initial search proved fruitless. In the decade of dial-up, not everything could be found in five seconds or less. Maybe I just wasn't as curious about the phrase as about the person who blurted it.

Plus, he was good-looking. Not *gorgeous*, but handsome enough that if he'd kept quiet and slouched less he could have been very popular in our high school. Though in that case I wouldn't have been interested, since I prided myself on not caring about popularity, or on actively avoiding it. The stuff I was into I'd gotten into on my own, or through television, or radio, actually I don't know, I can't remember—how I moved from one musical taste to another, or when I started reading serious books—I just remember that nobody else was into those things, or seemed to be, and while some part of me was probably sad about that, the prevailing part of me felt proud. So the fact that Jason Gustafson was not popular was in the plus column for me, while his dorkiness was in the minus column, though his actually being smart was in the plus, plus the fact that he was good-looking. The sum being that for a few years I'd been quietly curious. Toward me, he was aloof. Friendly, but not in a way that suggested interest. Maybe his lack of interest made him seem safe. Maybe it even made him attractive. Then one day out of nowhere he asked me to prom.

It was the only school dance I ever went to, and we never made it to the door. He took me to dinner, at least. Then it was still early, so we walked in the park around the fountains and talked for a *really* long time. Around and around the fountains. He kept hopping up on ledges, balancing for a second, then hopping back down. He talked about Buckminster Fuller, a name I didn't know. The first time you hear a name, it means nothing. Names only fill with meaning after you develop your own sense of the person behind them, unless the name itself is memorable, like, I don't know, *Buckminster Fuller?* Everything else about that conversation I've forgotten. I was too distracted by the staging. The whole conversation was overproduced. The fountains were nice, but the situation smelled strongly of a setup. Jason Gustafson was planning to make a move, and "Buckminster Fuller" was simply code for "The more I talk, the more impressed you will be." The fact that I knew very well what he was up to was what made it all so cringey. More off-putting than his condescension was his lack of subtlety. He must think me very silly indeed, I thought, if I'm not supposed to see *that* coming. And if he was unable to talk to me as a person, or, God forbid, a friend, then probably he wasn't seeing me as one either. Which was disappointing, because he wasn't a bad person. Or maybe he was, who could tell? I barely knew him. All I knew for sure was that he was a little bit of a moron.

He made his move and the rejection was awkward, but he recovered well. Then he said that a bunch of people were skipping prom to hang out in a field instead. That one I did *not* expect. He named some girls who were coming. I had imagined going to prom, but not with someone who was excited about skipping it, so we spent the night in a field, where they built a big fire. Jason brought his guitar, because of course he did. There was no booze, because all of those guys were straight-edge, or called themselves straight-edge even though there was nothing at all punk rock about them, just that they didn't drink. Which in high school was, admittedly, its own sort of legitimate rebellion. That whole night was fun. I had a good time. I missed out on prom, okay. I never went to another. I never went to any high school dances, ever. Does that bother me? I'm getting ponderous about all of this as if it bothers me. At the time, I barely cared at all. Why should I care now? It's like I'm inventing things to feel bad about.

Weird to think that was the beginning of our friendship, though. Fountains and Buckminster Fuller.

Because we *did* have a real friendship. Platonically challenged, but important to me.

I was in my office, talking about ideology. I nodded off. Speech-topic-wise, I think I left my office and mentally wandered into our bedroom without stopping to describe it.

Ladies and gentlemen, my bedroom. It has white walls, gray curtains, a dresser, side tables, and a king-sized bed. I sleep lightly on the side by the window, while Ed's body has created, over time, a man-shaped crater on the side by the door. As a result, there is a kind of dividing mound in the middle of the mattress, a rounded area where our bodies have not managed to smoosh the mattress down. It isn't symbolic of anything in our marriage. Only that Ed's body is like a furnace, and he can't sleep touching another person. He is cuddle-evasive. He gets too hot. I don't know if we are actually in this room yet, speech-topic-wise, but I know that whenever I did arrive at this room, I was going to talk more specifically about our contemporary moment, the kinds of stories we tell today and how they shape our reality. How the *forms* of the stories are as meaningful as the content, which is why we ought to think of the forms of stories as rhetorical, as elements of persuasion. In fact, that is almost all we do think about, when we think rhetorically: the history and ethics and efficacy of the forms of the stories we tell. Then I was going to tie all that back to Keynes's essay by a bit of transitional rigamarole that I'm sure will come easily tomorrow, when I'm actually standing in front of you saying all of this, but which I'm too tired to think about right now. It seems, ladies and gentlemen, that the weight of my tiredness is finally bearing down upon the roof of my insomnia. Soon that roof will collapse, this whole long night will be buried beneath it, and no ancient rhetorical memorization technique will be able to put it back together again. Everything I've thought tonight, every feeling I've felt, all the extensive mental meandering that's occurred here will end up being for nothing. But don't despair. Or do, if you want to. It's the same every night. Not just for me, for sleepless people all over the planet. The emotional effort spent. The mountains of worry wasted. I wonder if I will at least get through Jason Gustafson before it all comes crashing down.

After that night, he grew more attentive to me. Also, happily, more real. He would come by my locker to talk, or call me at home, and he spoke to me like I was a human being, not just some girl he could easily impress. Because he'd noticed what a lovely person I was deep down? Probably because I'd rejected him. High school emotions are about equal parts senseless and predictable. Unfortunately, I didn't have those feelings for *him* any longer. Mine had never been more than a crush of curiosity, tenuous and easily quashed. But I did like him. He was clever. He knew things. He could be arrogant, but he could also be fun. He played a few different instruments. He composed music. When he wasn't treating you as a conquest, he was an interesting guy.

So we became friends.

I liked his other friends, too. One of them, Paul, had a minivan. That old minivan! A moveable feast with cupholders. Minivans have always gotten an unfair rap, just big whale-shaped symbols of suburban normalcy, but fill one up with a bunch of weirdo teenagers and—well, it's still suburban normalcy, but it doesn't feel that way to the weirdos inside. Inside that minivan we talked about things nobody around us talked about, listened to music nobody else listened to. We took road trips to semi-distant cities to see concerts and lectures and plays. If the question is when and how I became the person who is lying here tonight, the person who invested first her hopes and later her family's future in the promise of Western intellectual culture, who aspired to live the life of that culture, to breathe its air, then surely that story starts when our heroine first became aware of how much was "out there" that she didn't know. And that moment—which was actually many moments, starting at the end of junior year and continuing through the summer after high school—that moment mostly took place in the minivan of a guy named Paul, whose last name was Fredrickson.

Richardson?

The time we went to a lecture on Marshall McLuhan. Not *by* Marshall McLuhan, as I'd thought the whole time we were driving there, since it turned out he'd been dead for many years. It was a contemporary media scholar talking about McLuhan's predictions from the 1950s and '60s, how amazingly accurate they'd proven to be. Sort of like what I'm doing with Keynes tomorrow, I guess. Though on second thought that is an off-putting comparison, implying as it does that I've gone on to become a version of *that* guy, with his ponytail and corduroy shirt. That guy really saw McLuhan as a prophet, his main point was how spot-on McLuhan had been about *everything*, whereas I'm not really concerned with whether or not Keynes was "right." In fact, I'm arguing his rightness or wrongness is largely beside the point. So really what I'm doing tomorrow is nothing at all like the lecture I once attended in high school by a ponytailed media scholar in a corduroy shirt.

Marshall McLuhan had been ahead of his time, I was not surprised to learn. Everyone discussed in Paul's minivan was ahead of their time. But McLuhan actually was. He'd understood where technology was taking us long before we'd even invented many of the technologies that actually took us to the places where he thought we'd go. And he coined catchy, memorable phrases: "The medium is the message" or "We shape our tools and thereafter they shape us." At least I understood what those phrases meant—they meant our relationship to technology is more complicated than we think—unlike the utterly obscure "Agenbite of outwit," which, I learned that night, was also one of McLuhan's, though I still had no idea what it meant. He was very doom-and-gloom, Marshall McLuhan. Or seemed so to me. But I found it all smart, and I did not doubt that he was, in fact, right about everything. Not because the media scholar said so, but because to my high school self, any vision

"You don't need to do anything. What are you talking about? We're friends. We've only ever been friends."

"I feel like I messed things up."

"I mess things up all the time."

"With you."

"With me the only thing you've messed up is that you keep asking what you messed up. It's not good. I don't secretly enjoy it."

Did I secretly enjoy it?

I've always hated feeling that I have power. I like responsibility, but I hate the power that comes with it.

What the hell is wrong with me?

I do wonder, all these years later, with the benefit of hindsight, if Jason's romantic doggedness was useful to me, in the end. If his diminutive stature in the romantic aspect of our relationship made me feel tall not just there, but elsewhere. If his adulation bolstered my confidence and helped me to hold my own in the intellectual blather of the boymobile. If his pathetic crush made me smarter.

Wow, I think I just demeaned both of us.

Don't remember it like this.

You were friends.

Ed is nothing like Jason Gustafson. Or like other men. Men are not a type but a category. Ed is in the category, of course. But he has almost no aggression, which is atypical of the type. Sure, there are his occasional bouts of road rage, but those are more like tantrums. I wouldn't say he's passive, because he's always taking things on and making sure things work. His political organizing. His community work. And his own reading and research that he never shows me. But I would also not call him ambitious. I would say he's the opposite of that. He likes to work, but he doesn't give himself goals. He likes work for work's sake. He is basically allergic to ambition, which is admirable. A certain kind of admirable. On the far side of aggressive, passive, and ambitious lies a certain kind of admirable. Lies Ed.

I can hear him breathing there, next to Ali. Together our bodies are making an Ali sandwich. If I didn't have Ed, it would be an open-faced sandwich. I prefer open-faced sandwiches, actually, two slices of bread is just too much, the insides of the sandwich get lost in it. But I definitely would not prefer having Ali with no Ed.

Which is not to say that Ed is perfect, because perfect he is not. It would be easy to start naming ways the current Ed could be improved upon. How a little more ambition on Ed's part would be a really good thing right now. I could list for myself the limits of his admirability. I could easily dive into that, if I were short on topics.

But this isn't about Ed. This is the story of how I came to be here, the person I am in the place where I find myself. How none of it was inevitable, and much of it was simply dumb. I'm at the part where I set off for college, get lonely, then visit Jason Gustafson in Texas.

It started in *Ulysses* class, about halfway through the semester. "Agenbite of inwit," said the professor. Did I hear that right? "The Agenbite of inwit," he said, "from the Middle English. The again-bite of inner wit, or more simply, the remorse of consciousness." Or, more simply still, if I understood correctly, a fancy term for the human conscience. The phrase runs through Joyce's novel like tracer dye. Of great thematic import, yadda yadda. The professor gave a whole long lecture about it. Me of course thinking immediately and for the entire period about that time in high school strings practice when I told Jason Gustafson to buy his own electronic tuner, because I was tired of lending him mine. "Agenbite of outwit," he'd said. Which I'd later found out was from Marshall McLuhan, and which now, in *Ulysses* class, I saw was actually a reference, by McLuhan, to James Joyce. Part of a vast web of reference I'd been caught in without knowing it. That this web seemed to be made exclusively of dead white men did not exactly inspire me, but the *coincidence* was exciting. I hadn't even realized McLuhan's phrase was a pun! Had Jason Gustafson known it was a pun? Had Jason Gustafson ever read *Ulysses*? At least it was supposed to be a pun; in truth, I couldn't quite figure out how the pun worked. How did McLuhan expect us to move logically from the "remorse of consciousness" to our passion for technology, or our full-throated embrace of our robot future, or whatever he intended "Agenbite of outwit" to mean? How was anyone supposed to get from Joyce's meaning to McLuhan's just by flipping the "in" to "out"? Until at some point the professor asked if I had something I wanted to add, because apparently I'd had a weird busy look on my face all through his lecture.

Back in the dorm, I called Jason Gustafson.

Holy shit, how *was* I?

Had it really been months?

It was great to hear from me.

Texas was good.

College was good.

He was probably going to study engineering.

That last one surprised me, since his dad had been an engineer, and Jason had once told me how happy his dad was on the day he'd retired. How shocked he, Jason, was to learn that for all those years his dad had hated his job. When I reminded him of this story, he said that his dad had been a chemical engineer, while he was studying electrical engineering. It seemed a meaningful distinction to him. And I was bursting to tell him about "Agenbite of inwit," so I dropped it.

He remembered McLuhan's phrase, and our once having talked about it in Paul's van. He didn't remember saying it to me in strings practice. It was one of those things he must have picked up along the way. He loved that I'd remembered all of that, though, and could see why I'd been pleased to stumble onto this connection. How funny it must have been when the prof called on me! He'd never actually read *Ulysses*, though he'd always been meaning to—and so on. Not a profound conversation, but it was nice to hear his voice. To think about high school, which already seemed so long ago. And which I guess I missed more than I'd realized. I'd called Jason to share an intellectual connection, but maybe it was an emotional connection I was really looking for. College life was full of the electric thrill of learning. I missed the oddball camaraderie of Paul Whatshisname's minivan.

The second half of that semester was rougher than the first. Everyone had settled into their friendships, and I was over-enrolled. I was alone a lot, in the library or the dorm. I called Jason only a couple more times. They weren't important calls, or even very substantive, but they kept my old life present in my mind. Which I guess allowed me to develop, amid the stresses of that semester, quite a lot of nostalgia for my recent past. And presumably it was this nostalgia, more than the phone calls, that led me to get on a plane after finals to visit Jason in Texas. It was the nostalgia that led me to think I had feelings for him, or that I *might* have something other than strictly friendly feelings toward him, though whether or not these feelings were real, I couldn't tell. On top of which, he had a girlfriend now, so ostensibly I was just visiting as a friend.

Somehow he'd skipped dorm life and was living in a ratty ranch-style house with slacker roommates and a pool. The surprise of the warm weather. The sticky heat. From the minute I arrived, I had no idea why I'd gone there. They were in the midst of their own finals week, and even though finals at Jason's school seemed markedly more relaxed than at mine, it still meant nobody was free to go anywhere or do anything fun.

For three days, I read books, sat in the local diner, and talked at his kitchen table with people I didn't know. His girlfriend was nice to me, and I felt bad that I found her so boring. In response to her niceness, all I could think was how dull she was. Not that she needed to impress me. If anything, I was a little impressed that Jason was by all appearances a good, dedicated boyfriend to this very dull person. And it turned out I wasn't at all attracted to him. Spending time with him was nice, but awkward. It was clear from the start that he'd changed as much as I had, only in a different direction.

His house was on the corner of a street that ended about ten houses down in a cul-de-sac, and whenever he found time to get away from his books and his friends and his girlfriend, we would walk to the cul-de-sac and back. Our conversations were fine, but generic. Generic but also *vague*. Everything about Jason's life seemed vague to me. Everything about my being there. As if something needed to be figured out, but neither of us could say what it was, because we couldn't figure it out, and because it was different for each of us. We were keeping each other company while we tried to figure out our own weird feelings.

"So," he'd say, "college is awesome?"

"College *is* awesome. I can't believe how great college is. So much better than high school. Not even comparable, a totally different world. Like I traded in my high school self and got an upgrade, and so did everybody else, so now we're these new people and there's a sense of possibility to it. Not like 'reinvention,' but more like everything before was just practice. We spent all those years running sprints up and down the field and now we finally get to play. Aren't you liking it? Things seem good here."

"Oh, things are great. I like what I'm doing. I have a cool girlfriend. She likes you a lot, by the way."

"Yeah, she's cool."

"I like the house. Everybody's great. Plus, pool."

"The pool is a plus."

"I know what you mean, though. Not reinvention but more like a do-over. You know Plato's Myth of Er?" He proceeded to tell me: "Er was this Greek soldier who died and went to the afterlife, where his soul got in line with other souls to be judged and sent back to Earth in some different form. The souls proceeded through the usual steps, though Er sort of hung back watching. Eventually, they all came to the final judgment, and Er saw the other souls choose what form to return as, like you could be a fish or a bird or an emperor, though whatever you chose had good and bad consequences, which you couldn't know ahead of time. Then on the way out the gate, all the souls drank magic water to make them forget their pasts, but Er didn't drink the water, so he woke up alive as himself, able to remember all of it. During freshman orientation there was a thing where everybody had to say what being in college felt like. I said I felt like Er, though I'm pretty sure nobody knew what I was talking about."

I remember that story because it surprised me. I hadn't realized until then how much my sense of Jason had changed. Somehow, I'd forgotten how pretentious he could be, and that he actually knew things.

On my last night, which was also the last day of their finals, they threw a party at the house. I spent most of the night sitting alone under the palm trees on the far side of the pool, in the warm breeze, listening to the palm leaves rustle. Fronds. The breeze through the trees made a sound like a large bin of rice being sifted back and forth. I felt bad being antisocial, but by then I'd reached my quota for talking with people I would never see again. I just wanted to go home.

At some point Jason came out with beers and sat next to me. He drank beer now, which was disappointing. Then again, so did I. It was disappointing that both of us now drank beer. In high school, not drinking had felt special, like you were making a statement about the clichéd expectations of American youth. In college, beer was just beer. There were different statements to make. After some chitchat, I asked about his engineering classes, a topic we'd somehow avoided over the previous days, perhaps intuiting that it would lead to nothing good. I brought up the story about his dad.

"Aren't you worried your life will end up being just sort of normal and boring?" I said. I could hear how presumptuous this sounded, but at the time it seemed important to say.

Jason looked surprised. "As opposed to what?"

Maybe something you actually care about? I wanted to say. Maybe something you ever once expressed interest in the entire time we were friends?

"I always thought you'd pursue music," I said.

He made a sour face, as if pursuing music had never occurred to him, even though in high school he'd been fairly serious about it. He finished his beer.

"So, what's *your* plan?" he said. "Do you even have one?" He was irked.

"My plan is to have no plan." This was true, and something I'd told myself when I needed to be reminded, but it sounded less impressive when I said it out loud.

"Yeah, that was my plan in high school," he said, looking off.

What did *that* mean? I honestly didn't know. Was he saying that my attitude was immature? Or was he criticizing himself, saying he felt stuck on a path he didn't want because he hadn't worked hard enough in high school?

Then he turned to me and said: "Why did you come down here, Abby? It's like you want me to tell you how great you are. You mope around. You sit out here by yourself, and when I come to join you, to save you from whatever pity party you're throwing yourself, you tell me my life is going to be boring. What the hell? You're not even nice to my girlfriend, who by the way has been damn understanding about the girl I used to have a crush on coming to stay with me. Also, not that I owe you any sort of explanation, but I find electrical engineering really interesting. Do you even know what electrical engineers do? Forget it. It doesn't matter. You're just really messed up. I mean, be as messed up as you want, but leave me out of it." He allowed me a solidly awkward ten seconds to respond, then got up and went back to the party.

For a while I sat looking across the pool at those clusters of people I didn't know. His outburst had shaken me, and being shaken made me notice, suddenly, finally, how fragile I'd become. I'd never thought of myself as fragile. It was in college that I started struggling with all of that. Nor had I thought those things about myself, any of the things Jason had just said to me.

In hindsight, I have no idea what was actually going on with Jason in that conversation, how much of his animosity had to do with me and how much was about his own life and decisions. Not that it mattered. Whatever was going on in his head, he certainly wasn't wrong about me, and by the time I boarded my flight the next day, I'd come to some awful conclusions. Everything Jason had said was true. *I* was the one who didn't make sense. I'd gone there wanting confirmation from him, some kind of confirmation. Either from him, or at his expense. I wanted to feel reassured, or to know that I was "right." College was kind of awful, actually. I'd been caught up in myself, my grand entrance to humanity. But humanity was just a bunch of people I didn't know standing on the far side of a pool, and none of them seemed very impressed. The life of the mind—was that what this was? "Agenbite of outwit" wasn't even a good pun. Everything I'd been doing, here at the start of adulthood, seemed suddenly kind of cheap. As if knowledge was a trick you played on yourself, a riddle to solve. The problem with riddles is they lose their interest the moment you solve them. Academia was a web of white guys you don't even realize you're caught in. One semester into undergrad, I was already on the wrong path.

All of which would have been just another stupid mood, not worth remembering at all, let alone all these eons later, were it not for the fact that *that* was the moment.

That was when I decided to major in economics.

It was that particular Abigail—a floundering mess on a homebound flight, shaken by a tough semester and an awkward trip to Texas into doubting her own optimism, questioning her own enthusiasm, feeling pretentious and shitty and wanting to escape herself by taking what she assumed would be the most practical path—who made that enormous life-shaping decision. Having no idea, of course, where it would lead.

The problem with lacking ambition is that even as he lies here making very little noise, so peaceful it's frankly annoying, like it's not enough to be "a good husband" sixteen hours a day, he has to log the other eight as well—the problem, *Ed*, is that in propping me up with all your glorious support, you also put mountains of *pressure* on me. Pressure to stay calm, to sleep well, to be brilliant, and to succeed at a career which, when it happens to tank, leaves me with mountains of *blame* as well.

At least in my mind it does, and my mind is where the blame does all the damage.

I love that you volunteer your time. I admire that you don't care about conventional measures of worldly success, and it was a great help to have you taking care of Ali while I was reading and researching and writing. You were very supportive, leaving me alone when I needed to work, or letting me vent when I needed that. But it was six, almost seven *years*, during which you could have been doing more for yourself. You could have built a career. Maybe not a career you wanted, but you could have been a high school teacher by now. You could have been a college administrator, one of those secondary deans who labor under piles of paperwork but at least cash a regular paycheck. You didn't need to be so content with a low-paying adjunct position, volunteer organizing, and hobbyistic scholarship. You didn't need to be so damn happy with your life, or place so much carefree faith in my success. Even assuming I was going to get tenure, which was always, *always* a question, still you could have wanted more for *yourself*, a more grown-up role in society. Or at least more lucrative! How different our lives would be now if only you had wanted these things. Instead, you lie here like a martyr ready to "support" me some more, telling me everything will be fine and I don't need to worry, that if I don't find another job, you'll find one, but what kind of job are you going find, Ed? The kind you didn't bother to get over the past six almost seven years? The kind you said would make you feel trapped, which wasn't how you wanted to spend the rest of your life? Lots of people have jobs that aren't exactly what they want to do, but they make something good out of it. And lots of people are stuck in jobs no one could possibly make good. Lots of people have no jobs at all. You and I aren't as fabulous as we think, Ed. The moral high ground is teeming with losers like us. Snobs. Thinking you're too good for crappy demeaning capitalism is a kind of snobbery. Snubbing societal norms is a kind of snobbery. Especially when there's a daughter involved. Tenure was never a given, Ed. Nothing is ever a given. Givens get taken. It's not like we didn't know.

In fact, *screw you*, Ed. Screw you and your countercultural exceptionalism, your good-guy privilege. How simple it all seems to you. How rational it all feels to you. How easygoing you are with Ali, and all the time you get to spend with her. I walk around full of shame for being the difficult one, but I can't help noticing I'm also carrying all the weight. Easy to be worry-free when everything in your life is simple. The historical simplicity of your life is a problem for us, Ed. You've always had people to fall back on, so deep-down you can't imagine a bad turn. You're incapable of even imagining it. You're like a climate denier, or a failed existentialist. Faced with the fact of our approaching bad days, you feel the need to put a smile on it. Everything's going to be fine, because for you everything always has been. From where you sit, it all looks easy. Anger looks easy, hope looks easy. Being a moral person looks remarkably easy. Despair, desolation, even ease looks easy. And optimism? Screw your optimism! Your struggle-free struggles. Your stress-free stress. Your patronizing levelheadedness and vapid enthusiasms. It was your brilliant idea to use the loci method, but you're not the one who has to give the fucking speech!

Beat of my heart in my head again, rush of oxygen to my brain, energy when energy is the last thing I need. *Energy at the wrong moment is inefficiency*, said Buckminster Fuller. Pollution is just inefficiency. The carbon dioxide smothering this planet is a potential fuel source waiting to be tapped. Those greenhouse gases are not a death sentence but a tremendous opportunity. Nothing is bad, everything is good, just being used badly. Hello, story of my life! "She had a lot of energy, but she used it badly," the epitaph will read. "She had energy to spare in the middle of the night, in the useless hours of the morning. Her insomnia energy could have fueled a small nation sustainably. She cared about the right things—she did!—but she did not pursue them as fully or as openly as she might have." Because caring about the right things isn't a recipe for success. In fact, one's own success is not typically considered one of the right things to care about. "She cared about the right things," the epitaph will read, "and yet she also cared about success. More than her husband did, anyway. He cared about the right things to a fault." Acoustical, also loving. "She married a man who cared about the right things, and she loved him and respected him and also found him a little disappointing.

It is a little disappointing to care about only the right things."
I will need a huge tombstone for all of this. "She cared about
the right things, but not *only* the right things, and she married
a man who cared about the right things, and she cared about
him, but not *only* about him." Or a very large urn? "She cared
about the right things but was not always steered by her desire
to do right, even if she was often, more often than not, steered
to do right. And at any rate she never tried to do anything
purposefully *wrong*. She had energy to spare but could not
always figure out the best way to use it. She tried plenty of
ways, but they did not always turn out to be the best. As with
our atmosphere's great big wonderful cache of

underutilized carbon dioxide, she failed to imagine the proper uses of herself that would have led to success rather than disaster." Maybe they'll just print it in a program for the funeral. A program could go on to several pages and everyone would read it, the way everyone always reads the programs at the symphony, because there's nothing else to do while you're sitting there. "She cared about the right things but not always at the right times, or rather it was at the right times but in the wrong situation, meaning that if she'd been 'herself' but in a different situation, things would probably have gone very well. But since she was 'herself' in the particular situation she was in, and since that situation did not match the times she was in, because the times were progressive and outward looking while the situation was a bunch of insular old men with antiquated ideas about everything, therefore matching her times meant, inevitably, that she did not match her situation, thus things did not go well at all." This is devolving into fatalism. Fate was at fault! Well, maybe it was, and she wasn't. "She worked hard and earnestly. She was neither lazy nor dumb." Maybe she only felt like she was at fault because that's how she always feels. Though sometimes she obviously feels the opposite. Like she isn't. And sometimes she can't decide—but for some reason feels the need to decide—whether she's at fault for her own fate, or isn't.

But when she asked herself how she got there, it was like walking into a mist. All she came up with was a handful of stories from her past, people she'd known who had shaped her. Who were responsible, to some extent, for the person she'd become. Emphasizing nurture because nature is really just yourself, whatever came in the original packaging, the basic model with whatever manufacturer defects. Though even nature you could blame on someone else. You could blame your parents! They were there the whole time. They natured, then they nurtured. In fact, it's all coming back to me now. The flood gates have opened, and the memories are rolling through. The original formative episode. The one I'm calling original. Calling formative. It's forming right here before me. Like something long buried in a hidden chamber, unearthed for the first time in millennia. A memory so old and dusty, so distant and thin that to even start remembering it I have to regress to the mind of a younger self. To the feeling of being however old that was, before responsibility, or worry, or crippling self-doubt. A child who lived inside her experiences. Like Ali? Like the innocence Ali's just starting to lose. Think of Ali and try to remember how that felt.

Heading home from the beach, our annual vacation, long dull hours in the olive station wagon, the back piled with luggage, the seat beside me stuffed with grocery bags stuffed with all our stuff. The boredom of small spaces, the exhaustion of endless sitting, but we were finally almost home, the "home stretch," when news came on the radio. A chemical explosion. A breach, a major incident. I understood what was happening but had no idea what it meant.

Soon a line of cars appeared on the far side of the highway, heading the other way. By then Mom and Dad were already arguing, though not with each other. They were agreeing with each other, but arguing with the world. They were having a petty squabble with the world. After hours in the car we'd finally reached the "home stretch," and now the world expected us to turn around?

Next we were home in the kitchen and I was sent to the basement to play. The more-or-less-finished basement with the musty couch and old toys. Fake wood paneling, mothball smell. That unconvincing coziness of carpet on a concrete floor. The radio was on in the kitchen and I could still hear my parents talking. The accident was miles from our house and the winds were blowing the cloud, or the current was carrying the sludge, or whatever it was—it was both—in the other direction. No official evacuation had been ordered, so even though all the neighbors were leaving, we didn't *have* to leave. And we'd just gotten home, goddammit. The vacation money was spent. The pet-sitter was halfway to her grandparents'. Where the hell were we supposed to go? If the cloud and the sludge were anywhere near, if they were headed toward rather than away from us, if the situation was *officially* dangerous, then, obviously, there'd be no question. But if it's all "recommendations," if nobody actually *orders* anything . . . At some point, I was sent to bed.

But the next day it was all still happening. The neighbors were still away, the radio rehearsed the same news, it was like the previous day had simply been extended, except that my parents had exhausted themselves worrying and we were obviously staying put. After breakfast I went back to the basement, bored. A week at the beach had transformed me into an outdoor animal, all that air and sand and sun still in my hair, my hands and feet. The situation outside was serious, dangerous, but there was also excitement in it, a sense of adventure, while here in the basement, we were all just sitting around. Me and the old blankets and stacks of board games and the kitchen appliances too big for the cupboards upstairs. Lunch was hours away yet. An eternity. To be stuck down here until then—was too awful. Which was why, after some unascertainable amount of time, I walked out the basement door. I think it was as simple as that. I was sick of the basement. I figured the backyard wasn't any less safe a place to play, though just in case I waved at the kitchen window. They saw me there, or I thought they did, or I told myself I thought so, running around and carrying on. I was pretty sure they waved back and were either fine with it or couldn't be bothered.

The woods at the bottom of the yard were, under normal circumstances, totally fair game for playing, and I couldn't see any reason why these current circumstances would be any different in terms of *that*. I had my stick fort down there, and my mud cliff, and my tree you could climb inside of. My god I was an awkward child. Already a loner back then. Never easy, never effortless, yet rather than force me into a lot of difficult social situations, my parents let me find happiness where I could, wherever or however I felt comfortable. I hope they know how lucky I was to have parents like them. I mean, I hope they know that I know that. Not that they weren't themselves prone to absurd bouts of worry and doubt, but they never took it out on me. If Ali had inherited my awkwardness, I wouldn't be nearly as understanding. I would crowd her with worries and advice, force her into poorly matched playdates, if only out of residual dread from my own childhood.

Where was I. The woods.

Not very deep, but long, a ribbon of trees that wound around the neighborhood. We owned only a small patch, but the woods themselves went on and on, and once you were in them, "private property" didn't mean much. Thomas More would have liked those woods. A world apart, an adventure all its own, a set of possibilities unbound by social expectation, and more so that day than ever. Because of the chemical cloud? That was scary and exciting. But the bigger deal, the much bigger deal from an adventure perspective, the thing that sent me questing beyond our property lines almost the instant I was out of eyeshot, was that everybody else, all of our neighbors, all their busy kids—were gone! Evacuated. No fear of stumbling into obnoxious boys or secretive teenagers. No angry old ladies shouting across their backyards. Not that I often ran into people out there, but I always knew that I might. It was the *threat* of people that weighed on me. Whereas the empty woods felt new and free and wild in a way it had never felt before.

Could any of this have happened? Could I really have left the house, set off into the woods, while my parents were tearing their hair out in the kitchen? I wasn't that sort of kid. Brave. Unless I was and just can't remember. But where else could such a memory have come from? A story I once read? A story that over the years I imagined myself into, replacing the setting with my own neighborhood, the characters with my parents and myself?

There was once a girl running around in the woods. These were woods she ran around in all the time, but due to a local evacuation in response to a catastrophic chemical spill, coupled with the unparalleled capacity for imaginative fantasy the girl had developed through years of playing alone, they were suddenly not the same woods at all. They became, as she moved through them, a world all their own—and there was nothing else, suddenly. With no people around to stop them, the trees spread outward, beyond the old boundaries. They engulfed the neighborhood, turned empty houses into ancient ruins, filled lawns with quicksand and vines, until the whole place became a jungle, the homes and yards and driveways, the lampposts and mailboxes. Everything familiar made strange. And she, the girl, felt no need whatsoever to contain her new freedom. Running through yards, over porches and patios. Could this have happened? Standing in driveways or in the middle of the street. Peering in windows. Messing with swing sets. It happened and it lasted an immeasurable span, an incalculable spell. The street was a river and the current swift. If you stepped out into it, it carried you along. It flowed up the hill seven houses down and over the other side. From there it flowed on to parts of the neighborhood the girl had never traveled by herself—but by then she had already decided to keep going. She'd gone farther before with her dad, so it wasn't that big a deal. Nothing about any of this had to be a big deal. Your mind makes it a big deal. You just have to decide that it isn't.

Distances always seem longer when you're heading out. Especially heading out for the first time, going anywhere takes forever. That girl knew perfectly well what she was up to. She didn't know it in the way that *I* know it, she couldn't fit the experience into a much larger life-puzzle, but she knew, she knew. That she was alone, out there, in a way that was exciting. That the freedom she was experiencing was not simple, or simply fun, but also serious, complex. An experience of strength, of being in control of herself and her surroundings. Her jungle fantasy was thrilling, but there was also, adjacent to it, this other feeling. A personal space opening up inside.

Is this a coming-of-age story?

She had in mind that she would loop the whole way around the neighborhood and get as far as the creek, the spot near the neighborhood entrance where the creek turned up toward the road, where people sat or fished and a few times a year the road flooded. It was a spot her family drove past every day, but she'd never stopped or stood there. In truth, she was only mildly curious about it. It was just a place to end up.

She'd not gotten nearly as far as that, however, when a voice yelled:

"Hey!"

The girl jumped.

Standing in a yard was another girl from her school, from a grade younger, who she'd seen in the hallway but never spoken to. Someone she'd wondered about. Her name was— Becky? Meredith? Back then I would have known. I see that girl standing there, with her giant house behind her. A huge cube of white siding and extra-large windows, one of those cheesy monstrosities that rich Christians live in, or that I've always for some reason imagined rich Christians living in.

"I've seen you in school," the girl says to me.

"Me too," I say.

"You didn't evacuate?" she asks.

"We just got back from the beach," I say. Something like that.

"My dad says it's all baloney. Where do you live?"

"The other side of the neighborhood."

"Your parents let you run around? I have to stay in the yard."

"Nobody's around. You can run all over."

And I told her, then, all the things I'd been doing. The patios, the swing sets. Probably I left out the imaginative make-believe aspects and focused on the anarchic rule-breaking. In fact I have a memory of doing just that, of *noticing* that shift, all my sumptuous imaginative fantasy booted out, along with everything else I was feeling, my burgeoning awareness of freedom and control, my entire complex of thoughts and emotions, all of it suddenly booted by an onrush of preadolescent awareness, an overpowering need to impress this girl.

This is definitely a coming-of-age story. Or a *finally-coming-of-age* story. An awkwardly-groping-for-maturity story. An other-people-ruin-everything story? A you're-the-one-who-ruins-everything-other-people-are-just-being-themselves story. A story about a girl whose name I no longer remember, who in that moment was the only other life-form on the planet, except that she was also, simultaneously, a girl from school who I wanted to impress.

She listened to my adventures and she did, in fact, seem impressed. And after that we talked for a long time. She didn't leave her yard. I forgot my other plans. Probably we talked about school, and people we both knew, the fact that everybody was gone, how weird that was. How boring the radio was being. How parents worry about everything. The white clouds in the blue sky did not look like chemical clouds, not that I knew what chemical clouds looked like, but they looked like regular marshmallow clouds, the kind you sit in the grass and guess at. We sat in the grass. At some point I thought: *This girl likes me*. She said: "You're funny." The sudden rush of optimism you get when you meet someone on the far forbidden side of the neighborhood and you simply *hit it off*.

Thinking later, on the way home, that I never "hit it off" with anyone. And what are the chances I'd find such a person when everybody else was gone? The only person around— turns out to be the good one! Which made sense, though.

Because having a lot of people around didn't help you find friends. Most of those "potential friends" were more like obstacles to finding real ones. They were the kids you had to get along with, who made you feel like something was wrong with you because you didn't like the things they liked or find the same jokes funny. And there were so many of those kids that it really did seem sometimes, a lot of times, that the point of your life was to learn to be like them. But the truth was, the thing that was true but different from what they tell you, was that your actual friends, the kids who were like you or made you feel that the way you were made sense—those kids were out there, waiting to be found. And the good news is that you find them, you do, once all those other kids get out of the way.

I liked a girl who liked me!

—walk-skipping through a shower of happiness. My morning adventures all but forgotten as I projected myself into an imaginary future, a future in which I had a best friend who was excited to talk to me and liked the things I liked. Who came over for playdates or met up at the pool. From now on, elementary school would be less lonely, even though she was in a different class, because having a best friend would give me confidence to make others, and it all adds up. Confidence breeds confidence, the effects of causes become the causes of later effects. Probably my younger self did not think in exactly these terms, but then again, maybe she did. Maybe I was already imagining what middle school would be like for a more confident Abby. Friends would be in school clubs and would ask me to join.

wonders had seemed possible suddenly weren't, and I realized too late that I couldn't arrange to see that girl without telling my parents how we'd met and what I'd done—the sneaking out, the wandering off—and *getting in trouble with my parents* was the worst thing I could imagine. Worse than chemical spills and evacuations. Worse than all the long-term health and ecological impacts of an environmental catastrophe, which frankly I could not have imagined at all. I chose not to tell my parents about the girl because they would have been angry and disappointed, and because my childhood imagination, so free in other ways, could not see beyond their anger to what now seems absurdly obvious: that they would have gotten over it, and once they'd gotten over it, would have been happy I'd made a friend. Instead, I sulked in my room, and the summer passed, and by the time school started up again, the girl had forgotten about me. Or she'd decided to forget. I walked up to her one day in the hall and it was like she didn't know who I was. She was surrounded by her friends and they all looked at me like I was crazy. This is an *awful* story. Why are you telling yourself this awful fucking story?

I also know *what happened* in the more general sense, that I'm lying here next to Ed and Ali, listening to the air conditioner. I know the events of my life in all the years between that moment and this one. *My life* is what's about to happen to that happy girl back there on the sidewalk—she just doesn't know it yet. Maybe that's why this story, which seemed so important a minute ago, but which has since revealed itself to have agreed to be here—STOP *I can't stop*—I must really have managed to hide it or they'd have taken off long ago, how I managed to get this far without everyone seeing what a phony I am is a total mystery, I didn't get tenure because I never should have been offered that job in the first place, everything I've thought has been thought by other people and better, I am not worth anything, I am seriously not worth a thing. Thoughts that are not new but are always, every time they revisit me, *infuriatingly convincing*, no matter how many times I've thought them or what I objectively know. Convincing and so scary I can't lie still for them, my feet muscles clench, my legs clench, clench against the venom, like some sort of self-poisoning organism, the animal that adapts to survive itself, it develops a soundproof skull so no one can hear its heartbeat clanging around in its head, it goes stiff with tensing and its hands turn to claws not for attack or defense but to hold it all in, its skin gets hot, it molts like a bug or lizard but since it can't shake it off it just sits in it, this cellophane skin, this suffocating crust, the raw exposed underskin now pink and angry, the whole creature like some ugly pink pulsing *thing* STOP its jaws clench, arms, claws on the mattress *please* that creature is you and you have faced these feelings before, you've muscled through them many times, you know all the phrases to recite to yourself but you also know that nothing you tell yourself will convince you, because anything you say will have to compete with everything you already think, and dark loathsome thoughts are always the most convincing. Locked in your brain with your various versions, the mommy-mummy dress-up-dummy bad-friend hovering-mother, all the things you are all the things you've been all the things you still need to deal with, you battle it out, you have to *you don't* I always do *you can stop* since when *you can choose to* as if it's that easy *no one said easy* but I can try *yes* I can tell myself to STOP

STOP

STOP

STOP

Are you done?

Yes, I'm done.

You're okay?

Yes.

You're sure you're okay?

I'm sure.

Good.

Now tell yourself what you know.

My problems are important and so is all the rest. The past and future, the planet and the people.

Sometimes the bravest thing you can do is lie still. Other times—it isn't.

There are ways I could improve myself, but I am also capable. I am not powerless. I am not my past.

I am not the product of other people, not Maggie, or Evelyn, or Ed. I made myself and, if I choose to, I can change. I can imagine myself differently. I can *make the imagination real*. Who said that? Maybe I did. Not every phrase in my brain belongs to someone else.

Having a child doesn't make you better than other people, but it did make me better than myself. It made me less self-absorbed, if only because I was suddenly absorbed with Ali. Being absorbed with someone other than yourself must be better than being absorbed with only yourself, but it's still just one other person, and what needs to happen, what I think is supposed to happen in the progress to becoming a better human is that being a wife to Ed and a mom to Ali is not an end but part of a process, to train me for greater things. Finding yourself no longer alone at the center of your moral universe is only admirable if it helps you imagine committing yourself in other ways, to other things, other than yourself. That seems right. That is the person I want to be. God, I hope I remember this in the morning.

Politics will change. Climate change won't. Social instability is a precondition of progress. Losing tenure has no bright side, but it isn't an end. As Ali gets bigger and needs me less, the point must be for me to get bigger as well, not to regress into solipsism but to follow the path that parenthood opened.

Maybe tonight has been more than just another bout of pointless worry, forgotten forever when the sun comes up. Maybe the sense I've had all night that I've arrived at a juncture, a turning point, that all these thoughts and feelings *mean* something—maybe that is not just my insomnia playing tricks. It's real. I don't need to be afraid of forgetting. I know that I won't forget. Tomorrow I'll remember how my imagination fought itself, and how I took charge of myself, and I will change.

What sort of change?

I will worry less about my own stability and security, worry less about Ali, who is amazing and competent. I will treat myself better, and by extension will treat others better. I will have a brave mind. Keynes was never a parent. He looked for courage in other places, found generosity in thinking. It's what he came to thinking for. To solve problems but also to live in the generosity of the mind and the imagination. That is not economics or scholarship, that is just being a thinking person in the world.

I will revisit writers who have mattered to me. Naomi Klein on reconceiving realism. Saidiya Hartman on radical imagination. Irene van Staveren on economic pluralism. It's not how you fit, but what you can contribute. *It is amazing what you can accomplish if you don't care who gets the credit,* said Obama, quoting Truman, I think. I will probably always crave credit from other people, but at the very least I need approval from *myself*, and the only way back there is to take my love for Ali and Ed and extend it outward. Not to assholes, but to everyone else. Make sure to remember this in the morning!

And I will refocus on the good things I already do. I'll remember that I got into teaching because I really like teaching, not colleagues and career advancement but teaching itself. Teaching is a way to feel a part of things and to contribute to other people's lives, just as my own teachers contributed to mine. I don't need to be famous. I don't have to be a reincarnation of Keynes. Or Robinson. Kate Raworth. Raj Chetty. I'd be terrible at fame anyway. It's only in its absence that fame appeals to me, in the paranoia petri dish of not having any. But *teaching* I'm good at and enjoy. I will find a job at a less fancy school, smart, not snobby, where I can focus more on students, less on "success." My new job will turn out to have as many downsides as my previous job, probably more, and for a lower salary, but it will also have upsides, or I will find some, if I can manage to remember what I care about.

This night has been too long. I knew it would be long, but not *this* long. I am much too tired. But I also know that it's almost over. I feel exhausted relief that this night is nearly done, because when it's done, something new will begin. Something new is coming whether I want it or not, but I won't be afraid, I won't sit back and watch, I am not really so old, how old I am doesn't matter. I am tired of being mean to myself. I am tired of being nice to myself. Restlessness is a lack of trust, and I trust myself enough to be tired. A sameness descends over everything, a weary stillness—over everything. My memory is put to bed. My thoughts are put to bed. Only my imagination continues to stir. In my imagination, I've arrived at Ali's bedroom. Last room on the list. Final portion of the talk. Okay let's get it over with.

The bed we bought at IKEA, which we'll never do again because Ed swore a barn door putting it together and it's never been completely right. There's a creak any time you sit on it, or roll over. She's gotten too big for it anyway. She needs a new one soon. Maybe we can give it away when we move.

The giant stuffed giraffe she got from Ed's parents for her sixth birthday that has taken up the whole far corner ever since. How will we ever get rid of *that*? Big things are so much harder to throw away than small things. Because they cost more? Because they displace more of your life. Because you are forced to live not just *with* but *around* them. It's the inconvenience of big things that makes us hold on to them, the daily concessions we make to keep these big things around, the sense of *investment* that makes us feel as if, somehow, someday, it ought to pay off. Am I still talking about a stuffed giraffe? What else could I be talking about? Nothing. A stuffed giraffe.

The dresser is an heirloom, if an heirloom can be a piece of junk. I had it in the basement packed with old books, but Ed pulled it out and repainted it. Four full coats of white to cover that ugly yellow. Then he added these adorable details, little golden vines winding all around it, and purple flowers. I loved that he didn't make the vines green. The gold seemed inspired, extra special, magical, so it was a letdown when he admitted that he just didn't have any green paint. Ed and his need to admit things. A happy accident, he called it. The same words we used about Ali, back when she was the accident we were happy about. We kept putting it off, thinking we weren't ready, that we needed to get our lives together first. By "lives" we meant our careers. By "our" we meant mine. Probably we would have put it off forever, because having a child is such a hard thing to imagine. In fact, you can't imagine it at all. Whatever you imagine isn't what it's like. It doesn't matter whether people try to describe it, or warn you. To our infinite credit, we embraced the accident when it came. We called it happy. Otherwise, where would we be now? Nowhere. We would be truly nowhere in a not-good way if the accident called Ali hadn't happened, and if we hadn't been self-aware enough, when it did, to know that without this accident we'd have postponed that happiness indefinitely, procrastinating ourselves into an unknown but undoubtedly dismal future.

Though, with no Ali to take care of, I might have gotten tenure. All that extra time. I mean, who knows? And realistically I would not *miss* Ali, since she would never have existed. In which case I would have tenure and no regrets. I'd have general regrets of the things-I-never-did type, but none that I could put a name to. Ed and I would be one of those cool

The ceramic kitten lamp with the purple shade.

How purple is not just her favorite color but also her favorite flavor. Blueberry pie. Grape popsicles.

Her shelf of all the books she loves, Beatrix Potter and C. S. Lewis in hardcover stacked in with all the paperbacks. How early she was able to read, and all the stories she likes to write. How she'll sit in her room for hours working on drawings or stories to show us. Space heroines or banshees, fairy-tale rip-offs or the ordinary adventures of elementary school, whatever subjects she's into at the time. How I'll read her stories and talk with her about how wonderful they are, but feeling always secretly a little torn, a little worried that if I encourage her *too* much with her stories, she might take it seriously, might decide she's an artist or writer and never give any thought to being a scientist or doctor or, I don't know, lawyer? Professions that make money. Professions least likely to be replaced by robots over the next ten years. Though I suppose artists are equally unlikely to be replaced by robots, just that their wages are miserably low—none of which is the point. The point isn't that artists are poor, or that I am a coward on my daughter's behalf. The point is that "down the road" is so far from now that it's frankly absurd that anyone would even think about this or worry about it while reading one of her daughter's lovely stories. Ed's the same way, though. Even Ed. For all his easy-breezy "quality of life" stuff, when it comes to Ali, he worries much too far ahead. Whenever the slightest thing goes wrong for her, he mentally multiplies it across the length of her lifetime, imagining the direst outcomes. He never says so, but I know. I mean, it's not like we'd *do* anything. We'd never actually *limit* her. It's just one of those parental burdens we share that are too embarrassing to talk about.

Where was I. Bookshelf. All the adorable doodads she's neatly arranged on top. How many can you name.

Family photos. Soccer trophy. Pencils in a jar.

Clay shapes from pottery camp.

Fish fossil.

How she loves to wander around museum gift shops.

How she always wants to buy the weirdest things.

Snow globe. Wooden whistle.

Chinese finger trap.

Cup-and-ball contraption.

That's all I can think of.

Above the bookshelf, the framed drawing Maggie gave her of a little girl playing hopscotch. And the gallery of Ali's own "greatest hits" that Ed's taped around the wall. The one where she's smiling in the foreground and Ed's in the background, on a distant mountain, looking distraught with his shoes untied. The one where I'm some sort of warrior queen with enormous hair riding a dragon. The one she drew at the beach in Maine where we're all in a boat made of Swiss cheese. The one that's a family portrait except we're cats.

All of it bathed in light, for some reason. This whole room glowing in warm light. In much stronger light than you would ever find in this room in reality, even with all the lamps on and the curtains wide open. Ali's room. Her childhood bedroom. *They are all gone into the world of light,* wrote some poet somewhere. *They are all gone into the world of light, and I alone sit lingering here.* I'm sitting here, in my mind, on her creaky bed, lingering. Looking at her drawings, her bookshelf. Beatrix Potter and C. S. Lewis. Fortunately, I don't remember any more lines of that poem, or I'd be in danger of considerable nostalgia right now. Nostalgia for the present. You know you're in trouble when you're already missing what's right in front of you.

There's more in here. Things I've forgotten to include.

Her bedside table, which is also IKEA and cheap. Her childhood contains much more particleboard than mine did. Like at some point we stopped worrying about the trash heap and started designing for it.

The gummy animal decals stuck to her windowpane. Ed ordered them online after a bird flew into the glass with a horrible thud.

Her poster of that boy band she claims to like but never listens to.

And the random sampling of socks always hiding under the bed.

And that gaudy paper ball, that enormous spherical snowflake that hangs from her ceiling lamp. How could I forget that?

And the rag rug.

The sneakers.

The slippers.

And so on.
Purple light switch plate.
And so on.
Lots to hold on to, here.
Whole lots.
Pink plastic ruler.
Smudgy rainbow eraser.
Stickers on the headboard.
Sitting on her bed, lingering.
Time wounds all heels.

trying to give me some privacy. A moment to say goodbye to my daughter's childhood bedroom, which will be disappearing from our lives any moment now, because I didn't get tenure, but also simply because life moves on. Because even if we stayed, and nothing else changed, this bedroom would become an older girl's bedroom. He's a gentleman, Keynes. Giving me space. Waiting in there while I feel my feelings.

I open the closet door and at first it's just her clothes, a wall of clothes—she grows out of them so quickly—and a bunch of old toys and puzzles on the overhead shelf. Then I remember there's no lightbulb in this closet, so where's all this light coming from? It's coming from *behind* the clothes, not above, and when I push the front clothes to the side, sure enough, the closet is much bigger than I remembered. It goes back and back. The Lion, the Witch, and the Inexplicably Deep Closet. Perhaps it will lead to a forest. Possibly there will be Turkish delight, a dish that, when I was little, I for some reason imagined to be a kind of *meat*. Only later did I find out it's a dessert, rubbery sweet cubes in powder. No wonder the witch seemed so menacing to me, stuffing that boy Edmund with meat. Turning him into an addict, basically, for *meat*. Have some meat. Have some meat. What a sweet child you are. Aren't I beautiful? Long spindly fingers. Porcelain skin. Fur trim and velvet cushions. And something else, underneath. Adult. Sexual. Violent. Actually, that is a very strange book.

Hurry through the clothes and stumble into, not a forest, but a municipal hallway. The light turns out to be from

from being twisted into something useless, or worse, harmful, by people in power. He learned this lesson early, at the Paris Peace Conference after World War I, when Woodrow Wilson was promoting his Fourteen Points and his League of Nations and Keynes was pushing European debt forgiveness and lightening the massive reparations all the Allies wanted to pile onto Germany. Keynes came up with a weird but workable plan, his "Grand Scheme," which proposed that Germany would issue bonds to cover the cost of the reparations, but the bonds would be backed by the League of Nations, since nobody with any sense would buy bonds backed by dead-broke Germany. In other words, the bonds would be backed by the very people the reparations were being paid to, a sort of shell game by which everybody got paid, and a way of achieving the diplomatic peace Wilson had come to Paris promoting. But Wilson's people in Paris were all bankers, not economists but bankers, and the bankers couldn't stomach letting go of debts. Nor could they help noticing that the only member of the League of Nations with any money at the time was the U.S., which meant saying the League would back the bonds was really just saying the U.S. would pay for it. Nor were they eager to give up their newfound power over the global economy, even if it was to the League of Nations, which was Wilson's idea in the first place. So Keynes's Grand Scheme flopped, Germany got snowed under with impossible debt, fascism took hold, and we ended up in World War II. This being only one example of Keynes recognizing the massive scope of a problem and finding a wacky but workable solution, then watching it get squashed by more powerful people with vested interests who could never see past what they knew. Who failed to imagine possibilities beyond the meager few they'd been trained into. Like tenured professors. Do you know about tenured professors?

The point being that Keynes was well aware of the serious obstacles facing new ideas as they make their way into the world, but that didn't dissuade him. Simply having ideas wasn't enough. The purpose of an idea was to bring about positive change. So *that* struggle, the struggle for the practical application of good ideas, became the story of his life. And then it also became the story of his death, in the sense of his legacy, the life his ideas have lived since he died. Ideas have a life of their own, and like any other life, an idea's life tells a story, and like any story, the story of an idea is happy or tragic depending on where it ends, or where the person telling the story decides to stop. In one sense, a life ends with death, but in another sense, it ends with forgetting. Ideas don't die, so mostly they end with forgetting. They're forgotten because they fail or because they succeed and become part of what we know. The new normal. To disappear into history or to disappear into normalcy—those are the options for ideas. Though sometimes ideas end without ever being known by more than one person in the first place. That is another option. And then there is the extraordinary case of Keynes, whose ideas, starting at his death and continuing to this day, have been twisted to fit just about any imaginable agenda. To justify government set of perfect ideas, of flawless stable structures, but a healthy diverse population of good ethical intelligent ambitious unpresumptuous individuals ready to take on anything. That *it is ideas which make people brave*, which is another quote from somewhere. *The only thing we have to fear is fear itself*, which FDR may very well have written after reading "Economic Possibilities for Our Grandchildren," just as the whole New Deal that followed seems lifted directly from the Keynes playbook. Not to say FDR *stole* Keynes's ideas, because nobody owns ideas, of course, and I have to think Keynes was nothing but happy to see his long-fought-for plans for government investment and public works finally put into action on a massive scale, even if it was in America, a country he'd never gotten along with very well.

But I was saying that even though Keynes would probably be disappointed by what's happened to his ideas since he died, how people in power have used his ideas to mean whatever they needed them to, to justify whatever schemes served their own ends, still I doubt he would be surprised. That was the point I was coming to, though I can't remember why I was coming to that point, or where I thought I would go from there, which is fine, though, maybe later I will remember it, but right now my attention is focused on a figure at the far end of this hallway, a man hurrying toward me, tall and lanky in gray tweed, watch fob, white mustache—it's him, it's Keynes!

"Oh, thank goodness," he says. "You need to see Pamela."

"Who the hell is Pamela?" I say, but jokingly, lightheart-edly, I'm so happy to see him.

"Who the 'hell' is Pamela?" he scowls. "Who the 'hell' is Pamela?"

He turns about-face and we continue in the direction I was going. He's a little out of breath from rushing to find me. "Pamela is running things," he says. "She has your itinerary."

"I have an itinerary?" I say. "I thought I was just giving a talk."

"You want to do it right, don't you?"

"Of course."

He seems miffed, though I don't understand why. Because I don't know Pamela? Because I questioned the itinerary?

"Or rather," I continue, hoping to paper over this little awkwardness by just ignoring it, "while I *do* want to 'do it right,' I don't want to *care* about it. I want to be okay with doing it badly, to protect myself in case that happens. I want to *act* as though I care, and *tell* myself I care, and do everything the way a person who cares would do it. But secretly, unbeknownst even to myself, I want to consider it all beneath me."

Keynes makes another face. My air of buoyancy seems flip to him. He doesn't see how nervous I am underneath, and it's really starting to bug me. Thank goodness the end of the hallway is here. Saved by the end of the hallway. Into a cavernous lobby with great glaring windows and a vast marble floor in the middle of which stands a small woman dressed in a blue skirt suit, her hair a gray bob. The whole enormous space of the lobby organizes itself around this woman. She is the rock at the center of everything. She's reading a clipboard but looks up as we approach.

"There you are," she says to Keynes.

Now he relaxes. He flourishes his arms toward me, like a waiter unveiling a flaming dessert. "Voilà."

"You'll be in the auditorium rather than the sanctuary," the woman, who obviously must be Pamela, tells me.

"There's a sanctuary?"

"Every religious complex has a sanctuary," she says, "though these days they are more often called auditoriums. Since our facility also includes both a cafeteria and a multi-use auditorium, we retain the older term for the worship space, to avoid confusion. The auditorium is right here behind me, but you don't want to go in there yet. No one's arrived. It's too early. If you look in there now, you'll see rows and rows of empty seats, and it will make you feel small. But don't worry," she says. "We always get a good turnout for these things. Last week we had former president Barack Obama."

"Obama was here?" I say. I'm surprised by how much comfort this brings me. Even just the name.

"He asked about you," she says, but she's turned back to Keynes.

"Oh?" says Keynes, delighted.

"He saw the poster and asked if you would be here."

"Yes, it would have been nice to see him."

Keynes knows Obama?

He and Pamela keep talking about it.

It's as if I'm not here, suddenly.

Aren't *I* the speaker?

What does the poster say?

"They're waiting in the library," Keynes says as he leads me down another hall, away from the lobby. I understand that "they" means Ed and Ali. They've come to hear my talk, and are waiting in the library.

"Is it a religious library?" is what comes out of my mouth.

"It's not *not* religious," he says.

"What does that even mean!" I'm tired of his weirdness.

"It's as much religious as it is a library."

"Keynes!"

He turns to me, suddenly irritated. "You could at least pretend to be happy about all of this."

Happy?

But I am happy, Keynes. I'm ecstatic. Can't you see? I'm the happiest I have ever been in my whole entire life, tagging along with you, being hustled around the halls of someplace I've never been instead of practicing a talk for which I am horrifically underprepared. Watching you schmooze it up with Pamela. How could I not be really super happy about every bit of this, Keynes? None of which I say out loud, because he is being so annoying.

"Earlier," I say, "I was thinking about the fate of ideas, what happens to them once they're out in the world. How you would feel *your* ideas have fared, Keynes. In my talk, I will probably stick to what you'd make of *the state of the world*, since that's what you wrote about in 'Economic Possibilities.' At the end of the talk, for example, in order to tie the end back to the beginning, I might ask rhetorically what you would think of how it's all turned out—the world—as compared to your so-called predictions. That seems the sort of thing an audience might relate to. But personally, while we're walking here, I'm more interested in what you think of what's happened to your ideas. Great success? Long slow failure?"

"I'm afraid I have to go," says Keynes, who's stopped in front of metal double doors. He's looking at his watch. He hasn't even been listening. "I told them I would be back sooner than this. Do you think you can get there from here? The quickest way would be to cut through the cafeteria. It's just beyond these doors. If you go through to the kitchen, then out the big door in the back, the library will be right across that hallway."

"Keynes!" I say. I stop him. "This is all too fast! I've never been here before. I haven't even finished practicing!"

"It's really very easy," he says. "Just through this door, across the cafeteria, a quick jaunt through the kitchen, and you're there."

"Wait," I say. "Wait!"

"What is it?"

I have his full attention.

"I don't think I should go into that empty cafeteria by myself" is what I say.

"Why on earth not?"

"I don't know anyone here. And large empty rooms make me nervous. High ceilings and all that empty air. It's like swimming in very deep water where you can't see the bottom and have no idea what might be down there. Do you understand?"

"I've never heard anything so ridiculous," mutters Keynes. He looks in the direction he needs to be going. "But if it worries you so much, be my guest and take the long way round."

This hallway is so like the others that I'm worried I've somehow gotten turned around. But there aren't any benches, and the right turn came where Keynes said it would. I just didn't realize, when he called this *the long way*, that it could possibly be this long. If I'd gone through the cafeteria, I would've been there by now, with Ed and Ali. But I had a bad feeling, and you have to trust those things. When I pictured the cafeteria, I imagined long rows of folding tables with blue and yellow chairs, the walls at floor level covered with bulletin boards, the bulletin boards full of flyers for bingo nights and guitar lessons. Above, it's thirty feet of yellow cinder block, with some basketball hoops at either end, then a strip of horizontal windows up along the ceiling. You push through a swinging metal door and the kitchen is gleaming cabinets, gleaming refrigerators and countertops, every surface stainless steel, like a hall of mirrors, a funhouse maze. Keynes gave permission, but he's not an official part of this place. What if someone was in there? What would I say?

But now I have a different feeling, now I'm angry, because Ed and Ali are waiting, probably wondering where I am, because I should have been there a long time ago. I should have listened to Keynes! But he shouldn't have left me, either. I'm worried I've gotten lost, that Ali and Ed don't know what's happening, and this is a feeling I don't need right now. This whole event is a huge mistake that I wish I'd never agreed to. It's not worth it. You put yourself out there, take on a thing like this, because you think that you should, or need to. Not because you want to, not at all because you *want* to, but because you are painfully aware of how greatly you would prefer to say no, to stay home, to climb into bed and read a book or watch something on your laptop, and you worry that's not healthy or good. Your natural inclinations seem counterproductive and *not good*. So you make yourself say yes, you force yourself, out of fear that you will live your whole life not "having lived" or whatever. But then here you are, living, and it's miserable! Not a meaningful corrective to your natural inclinations, just a terrible series of tortures with no redeeming value. I blame Keynes! How could he leave me? How could he think this would be okay? I feel so angry. But wait no here's something. The plaque says LIBRARY.

Okay, I'm here.

The plaque says LIBRARY but when I open the door, it's empty. The room is tiny, twenty by twenty, and I can see every inch of it immediately, because there aren't any shelves or books.

The wallpaper has images of bookshelves printed on it, full of images of books, and in the middle of the otherwise empty room is a leather chair for reading, with a little table beside it. A mass-market paperback on the side table. *This* is their library? I feel like laughing, if only for the emotional release. I can't believe I was nervous about giving a talk to these people.

In the opposite corner, there's a vertical window, only about a foot wide but stretching from the floor to the ceiling. It's the most library-like thing about this room, because it's just like the windows in my public library growing up. Seventies architecture. I walk over there. Outside is gray. A mist hovers over a dull-yellow field, treeless and flat. Through the mist, in the far distance, I can see the dark line of an ocean. Where are we? What ocean is that? I can make out, just barely, a solitary figure standing out there by the water. Yes, someone's there. I wonder what it would feel like to be out there right now. Gray chill, the spray, the smell. The beach wet and pebbly, strewn with dark-purple extraterrestrial sea vegetation. I would be wrapped in a heavy coat, and a knit hat, with black canvas shoes covered in little white clumps of wet sand. I would face the dark water, but at some point I would look back here, to this long tall window in the distance. The soft light through the window reminds me of warmth and comfort, carpeting and furniture. Ed and Ali are in there, and I'm going to join them soon, but I want to spend just one more minute out here in the cold, by the water. Then I remember that Ed and Ali aren't in that room. They were supposed to be, but they aren't.

I turn from the window to look for them, but a young man is standing in the doorway instead. He is tall and thin, with wispy dark hair and a boyish face. He doesn't look dangerous. More like nervous. No, I'm not afraid of him at all.

"Where are my husband and daughter?" I ask.

"Don't you know?" says the young man. "No wonder you're wasting time out here. They're all in the auditorium already. They've gone ahead and started the event."

"That's impossible," I say. "I'm the speaker!"

"You think I don't know that? They sent me to get you."

"Then you meant to say they're waiting for me."

"Oh, they waited," he says. "Finally they asked Keynes to do it. He's filling in until you get there."

"Keynes is giving my talk?"

"He said he knew it by heart. He said he'd gone over it with you."

"Yes, but he's not supposed to give it *for* me!"

"He thought you'd be happy about it. Apparently, you've been struggling?"

"He told you that?"

"He told everyone. We were all huddled there in the lobby, trying to figure out what to do. He said, 'Well, I would never want to impose, but the truth is she's done nothing but complain about this talk since we started working on it. I suspect she's actually hiding, in the hope that I will step in on her behalf. That is, I wouldn't be surprised.'"

"But he's the one who told me to come out here!"

"He told us that, too. That's why I've come looking for you. We're quite a ways from the auditorium, unfortunately. You understand that they had to move ahead."

"This is unbelievable," I say, suddenly realizing how much this talk means to me.

Another high school hallway, like every hallway I have ever known. The young man is slightly ahead, and I'm thinking: *How could this happen?* Keynes must have known that I didn't *mean* those things I said. I never completely *mean* anything. Words are always happening, but sometimes all they mean is that I needed them to come out. Surely Keynes understands that? Surely he knows that if I'm a little *casual* in how I speak to him, that's only because I trust him to not take me too seriously, or to know that even when I'm being serious, that doesn't mean everything I say is supposed to *count*. It's far too stressful when everything you're saying has to be exactly right all the time. To check yourself with every sentence. It's exhausting. I mean, that's what Ed is for. Having an Ed. Everybody gets one or several Eds to unload on. One or several Eds to speak to without having to *mean* everything. Keynes knows perfectly well he is one of my Eds. A secondary Ed. He knows perfectly well!

"I know Keynes," I say to the young man walking ahead of me. "He wouldn't betray me like this."

"He didn't 'betray' you," he says over his shoulder. "Only you would even consider that. The rest of us understand exactly what he's doing."

Stuart Mill says about Plato, that a true Platonist isn't someone who agrees with Plato's *opinions*, it's someone who interrogates life the way Plato did. Or it's like what I tell my students about politicians, that there's only one thing you can truly know about them, regardless of what they do and say. You can't know who they really are, or what they really think, or what they will do in the future, the only thing you can know is *how they speak to you*, what sorts of words they chose, what vernacular, what school-grade level of vocabulary. From this you can tell not who *they* are, but who they think *you* are. Do they think you're smart or do they think you are kind of a dummy? Do they think you need to be spoon-fed like a child, or whipped up into an adolescent frenzy, or do they think you can be reasoned with as an adult? Though on second thought this latter example is not at all similar to what I'm saying about amazing people and their ways of seeing. It's just a rhetoric tip. So many amazing people and the different ways they've contributed to humanity and all along all I've wanted was to be one of them. Not prizes or recognition, just to feel, myself, that I had joined that conversation. Had found something interesting to say and had said it before history moved on. History is always moving, of course, the world changes in different ways than however it changed previously, the changes change, they always do. There are too many factors, too many stories being told simultaneously, you try to skip and jump from one to the next, to fit yourself in among them, but there's only so much you can do, only so much you are good at doing, and whether or not the world wants capitalist macrostructure comes crashing down, individual agency and purpose get swallowed up by Fate, or by Deus, or more likely by Machina, whichever ominous authority you prefer to outsource your failures to, if you are anything like me, which, ladies and gentlemen, I sincerely hope you are not. No, I really sincerely hope that. I am here today speaking on topics like optimism and possibility and progress but the truth is I'm the last person you should listen to on any of that. The truth is I am mostly a terrible coward. If you need examples there are so many. Like the time Ali hid in the clothes rack at the department store, thinking she was being funny. It took me all of five seconds to start yelling. Ali, shocked, spills out of her hiding place, knocking about twenty pairs of pants on the floor. The look the cashier gave me. But I was so scared! Or the time we went to that fast-flowing creek with Ed's high school friend's family and all the kids were swimming back and forth across the creek. The water was fast and it flowed into enormous rocks about fifty feet downstream. Maybe Ali was a good enough swimmer but I wasn't taking any chances, *no way*. Ali was embarrassed. I think even Ed was embarrassed. Too bad! Or how nervous I always feel going to a protest march or rally. Not because of violence, I don't get as far as picturing actual violence, just the fear of putting myself out there is enough. Of asserting myself, my body, in an unsanctioned space. *The dangers of life are infinite, and among them is safety*, said Goethe, I think. Safety, stability—two good things that you can also overdo. Because wishing safety and stability for everyone doesn't actually give it to them. Wishing tenure for everyone doesn't make Universal Tenure a thing. And because *un*certainty is a part of living, too. Our friend Keynes wrote a whole book about it, the philosophy of uncertainty, maybe he's even been telling you about it, I have no idea what he's said to you so far. Ludwig Wittgenstein's *Tractatus* came along and rendered his book philosophically irrelevant, unfortunately for him, but later he used those same ideas to change economic theory forever, so there's that. Uncertainty is a fact of life and an important part of what makes life lively. Risk is the spirit of courage you bring to things you care about. On the other hand, risking your own safety and stability won't necessarily help anybody else, either. There's courage, then there's ill-conceived idealism. Being stripped of your own safety and stability might make you more empathetic to other people's problems, but more likely it will just make you mean. Too much money makes people greedy, and too much security makes people spineless, but a basic amount of money and security makes it much easier for a person to be decent and good. Which is one of the primary ethical arguments for universal basic income, by the way. Not that universal basic income needs ethical arguments. Universal basic income is the kind of no-brainer idea that appeals to anyone who understands it. The only thing standing in the way of universal basic income is that we don't already have it. If we had it, we wouldn't need to imagine it. If people were better at imagining it, we'd have had it a long time ago: a guaranteed income for everyone and, while we're at it, that drastically reduced workweek Keynes predicted.

kitchen or organizing a protest march, some form of social benefit you can see. It comes upon me suddenly, this fear, and of course I quickly remind myself that my subjects *do* matter, that striving to understand *how the world works* always matters, that even seemingly fanciful questions like the one I just asked are important, since how can you change if you don't know what to change *to*? Then I scold myself for letting my insecurities cause me to question my sense of purpose. Then I think about Keynes, and others like him, people who lived a life of the mind but also made a difference. Finally, when none of that works, when my pep talks fall flat and even my heroes fail me, I think of Ed, my husband Ed, and how at least I'm still better than *him*. Not that Ed is a bad person—that's not what I'm saying—but if anyone fits the mold for Keynes's 'grandchildren,' it's Ed. He has many admirable qualities, his political convictions, his organizing, his nice-guy-good-father stuff, but he also enjoys an awful lot of 'enlightened' leisure. Lately, his ease has been frankly infuriating, and I can't help feeling that his unflinching optimism represents a failure to take seriously the reality of our situation, but—*but*—in a Keynesian *alternate* dimension, I have to admit, Ed would be a model for us all. Ed the Keynesian man, the fittest to survive a utopian future, who unfortunately missed his moment. As did I, but differently. Maybe all of us missed our moments, and that's the problem with this world, that nobody fits. Maybe that's my finale. *Everybody in the world is in the wrong place at the wrong time.* The end. Thanks for coming. I'll take questions now. Of course, this last part I won't say, especially

"Oh, plenty."

"Earlier I was told there was 'plenty' of time," I say, my voice rising, "but then I was sent away and you all started without me!"

"Is that really what you want to say to me?" Pamela is unflinching. "Keynes assured me you'd want to use this time productively."

"I hate Keynes!"

"Now you're pouting."

"He led me down a bad path!"

"If you can't be productive," she says, "at least pretend."

"I shouldn't *have* to pretend."

"It's not a matter of should."

"Well, it should be."

"It's a matter of do."

"Do?"

"Finish."

"Finish!"

"It's the only option."

"No," I say—this one I know—"there are always other options."

"Not always," says Pamela.

"Maybe not *always*," I admit.

"Definitely not always," she says.

"But sometimes?"

"Yes."

"There are sometimes other options!"

"And sometimes not."

Before I can say anything else—I am out of things to say, but probably I would say something anyway—she offers to take me to the green room. They have a *green room*, of course they do, where I can catch my breath, collect my thoughts, get my act together. Fine, let's go to your green room. But when she turns around and opens the door in the wall behind her—

"*Mom!*" A whispered yell.

Ali? And Ed! They've been waiting behind this door the whole time.

"Where *were* you?" says Ali, all worked up. "Everybody's been looking all over!"

"I was looking for *you*," I say. "I trekked all the way out to that library."

"You call that place a library?" she says. Pitch-perfect delivery. My daughter.

"Oh my god I *love* you," I say.

Then I look at Ed.

"Showtime!" he says, doing jazz hands.

"Not yet!"

"No?"

"Apparently I still need to 'practice.'"

"Well, it's too late for that *now*," says Pamela, who for the first time appears visibly irked. So am I! I'm irked and flustered and an array of other unproductive emotions. She's mad because I've wasted all my so-called practice time, though obviously that makes *no* sense. The thirty seconds I just spent talking to Ali and Ed somehow used up my "plentiful" practice time? Pamela is in a huff. I go stiff, take on a coating. Ed and Ali lay their hands on me, to calm me down. Something that simple probably shouldn't work, but it does. The laying on of hands. Involuntary softening. "Keynes is almost finished," says Pamela. "I'll take you backstage."

"This isn't backstage?"

She groans. "You need to enter from the *back of the stage*."

Just let it go.

Of course, now that I'm finally back with my family, back again in the comfort of their company, I do not wish to separate from them, even for an instant. Yet it's precisely because of the warmth and reasonableness they bring me that I am able to acknowledge, now, that Pamela is right. I am the guest, this is the lecture, which I agreed to, which part of me has even looked forward to. In fact, I've been desperate to arrive! I *chose* this, is the thing to remember. I had reasons.

"I have to go do this," I tell Ali and Ed. "It will either go well or go poorly, or more likely it will go fine and be totally inconsequential, but either way, it will be over soon, and we can go home."

"Good luck!" says Ali.

"Good luck," says Ed.

Blown kisses as Pamela pulls me to the back of the stage, toward the narrow dark space between the cinder block wall and the rear curtain. It isn't really a passageway, just a storage space for theatrical junk, folded-up chairs and scraps of sets and props. The instant we step inside, everything around us dims, as if clouds just blew in. I no longer see Ali or Ed. Noises from the wings sound distant. As Pamela pulls me forward, there are obstacles in the way, murky objects of indiscernible purpose, and it keeps getting darker. Warmer. We must be getting close, though, because I can hear Keynes out there, his voice muffled by the heavy curtains. What is he saying? There's a buzzing in my ears, lightness in my legs, achy thud in my stomach. My fingertips scratching the surface of my palms creates an irritating tingle. Up ahead, two curtains overlap, letting through a sliver of light. Not a gap I can see out of, just this very thin line in the dark. When I get there, I will hear my name called, and I will walk out through those curtains onto the stage. The lights. The moment will take over. But here, it's like a cave. I can barely see. Pamela is a shadow. When she lets go of my arm, I'm alone. It's me.

I am thinking so many things.

ACKNOWLEDGMENTS

Most of the quotes in this book are cited by Abby herself, but four appear unattributed. "They are all gone into the world of light! / And I alone sit ling'ring here" is by the seventeenth-century Welsh poet Henry Vaughn. "History is the nightmare from which I am trying to awake" is James Joyce. "The barrier between oneself and one's knowledge of oneself is high indeed" belongs to James Baldwin. And "It is ideas which make people brave" is from Scottish novelist Alasdair Gray. Gray's full quote is "It is ideas which make people brave, ideas and love of course."

The French composer Abby prefers to Pauline Oliveros is Éliane Radigue.

This work owes a very large debt to Christian Anderson, a terrific person and enthusiastic economics professor who handed me, when we first met, for reasons I still can't imagine, a collection of essays on John Maynard Keynes by contemporary economists. That got this endeavor off the ground.

Abby's various intellectual adventures probably don't require a complete bibliography of sources, but for readers interested in Keynes's life, I recommend two excellent histories. Robert Skidelsky's *John Maynard Keynes, 1883–1946: Economist, Philosopher, Statesman* is the authoritative text, and was for me an invaluable resource. Zachary D. Carter's *The Price of Peace: Money, Democracy, and the Life of John Maynard Keynes* was, unfortunately for me, not published until I was well into this project, but it was still an important source for me, and a great pleasure to read.

One of the oddities of researching a fictional thesis I *thought* I'd made up was that I discovered along the way—as Abby discovers—that I was far from being the first person to think about economics in terms of rhetoric, utopia, and so on. Professor Dierdre McCloskey is the source that features most prominently in this novel, but there are many thinkers pushing our understanding of economics in new directions. Professor Irene van Staveren's *Alternative Ideas from 10 (Almost) Forgotten Economists* could not appear by title here, because it was published several years after this novel takes place, but I recommend it as a fun and engaging nonspecialist introduction to economic pluralism.

For allowing me to sponge off their various expertise, thank you to Ben Donnelly, Peter Schmelz, Joshua Cohen, Devin Johnston, Jessica Baran, and my brother, David.

Thanks to Kate Johnson, my agent, and Emily Burns, my editor—I'm so thankful for both of you! And all the good people at Grove.

I think of writing as a solitary activity, which is ridiculous, since there is always one other person here with me, reading, thinking, talking. Biggest thanks and love to Danielle Dutton.